LEFT

TO

HARM

(An Adele Sharp Mystery—Book Fifteen)

BLAKE PIERCE

Blake Pierce

Blake Pierce is the USA Today bestselling author of the RILEY PAGE mystery series, which includes seventeen books. Blake Pierce is also the author of the MACKENZIE WHITE mystery series, comprising fourteen books; of the AVERY BLACK mystery series, comprising six books; of the KERI LOCKE mystery series, comprising five books; of the MAKING OF RILEY PAIGE mystery series, comprising six books; of the KATE WISE mystery series, comprising seven books; of the CHLOE FINE psychological suspense mystery, comprising six books; of the JESSE HUNT psychological suspense thriller series, comprising twenty four books; of the AU PAIR psychological suspense thriller series, comprising three books; of the ZOE PRIME mystery series, comprising six books; of the ADELE SHARP mystery series, comprising sixteen books, of the EUROPEAN VOYAGE cozy mystery series, comprising four books; of the new LAURA FROST FBI suspense thriller, comprising nine books (and counting); of the new ELLA DARK FBI suspense thriller, comprising eleven books (and counting); of the A YEAR IN EUROPE cozy mystery series, comprising nine books, of the AVA GOLD mystery series, comprising six books (and counting); of the RACHEL GIFT mystery series, comprising eight books (and counting); of the VALERIE LAW mystery series, comprising nine books (and counting); of the PAIGE KING mystery series, comprising six books (and counting); of the MAY MOORE mystery series, comprising six books (and counting); and the CORA SHIELDS mystery series, comprising three books (and counting).

An avid reader and lifelong fan of the mystery and thriller genres, Blake loves to hear from you, so please feel free to visit www.blakepierceauthor.com to learn more and stay in touch.

HER LAST FEAR (Book #4)
HER LAST CHOICE (Book #5)
HER LAST BREATH (Book #6)
HER LAST MISTAKE (Book #7)
HER LAST DESIRE (Book #8)

AVA GOLD MYSTERY SERIES
CITY OF PREY (Book #1)
CITY OF FEAR (Book #2)
CITY OF BONES (Book #3)
CITY OF GHOSTS (Book #4)
CITY OF DEATH (Book #5)
CITY OF VICE (Book #6)

A YEAR IN EUROPE
A MURDER IN PARIS (Book #1)
DEATH IN FLORENCE (Book #2)
VENGEANCE IN VIENNA (Book #3)
A FATALITY IN SPAIN (Book #4)

ELLA DARK FBI SUSPENSE THRILLER
GIRL, ALONE (Book #1)
GIRL, TAKEN (Book #2)
GIRL, HUNTED (Book #3)
GIRL, SILENCED (Book #4)
GIRL, VANISHED (Book 5)
GIRL ERASED (Book #6)
GIRL, FORSAKEN (Book #7)
GIRL, TRAPPED (Book #8)
GIRL, EXPENDABLE (Book #9)
GIRL, ESCAPED (Book #10)
GIRL, HIS (Book #11)

LAURA FROST FBI SUSPENSE THRILLER
ALREADY GONE (Book #1)
ALREADY SEEN (Book #2)
ALREADY TRAPPED (Book #3)
ALREADY MISSING (Book #4)
ALREADY DEAD (Book #5)
ALREADY TAKEN (Book #6)
ALREADY CHOSEN (Book #7)

IF SHE FLED (Book #5)
IF SHE FEARED (Book #6)
IF SHE HEARD (Book #7)

THE MAKING OF RILEY PAIGE SERIES
WATCHING (Book #1)
WAITING (Book #2)
LURING (Book #3)
TAKING (Book #4)
STALKING (Book #5)
KILLING (Book #6)

RILEY PAIGE MYSTERY SERIES
ONCE GONE (Book #1)
ONCE TAKEN (Book #2)
ONCE CRAVED (Book #3)
ONCE LURED (Book #4)
ONCE HUNTED (Book #5)
ONCE PINED (Book #6)
ONCE FORSAKEN (Book #7)
ONCE COLD (Book #8)
ONCE STALKED (Book #9)
ONCE LOST (Book #10)
ONCE BURIED (Book #11)
ONCE BOUND (Book #12)
ONCE TRAPPED (Book #13)
ONCE DORMANT (Book #14)
ONCE SHUNNED (Book #15)
ONCE MISSED (Book #16)
ONCE CHOSEN (Book #17)

MACKENZIE WHITE MYSTERY SERIES
BEFORE HE KILLS (Book #1)
BEFORE HE SEES (Book #2)
BEFORE HE COVETS (Book #3)
BEFORE HE TAKES (Book #4)
BEFORE HE NEEDS (Book #5)
BEFORE HE FEELS (Book #6)
BEFORE HE SINS (Book #7)
BEFORE HE HUNTS (Book #8)
BEFORE HE PREYS (Book #9)

BEFORE HE LONGS (Book #10)
BEFORE HE LAPSES (Book #11)
BEFORE HE ENVIES (Book #12)
BEFORE HE STALKS (Book #13)
BEFORE HE HARMS (Book #14)

AVERY BLACK MYSTERY SERIES
CAUSE TO KILL (Book #1)
CAUSE TO RUN (Book #2)
CAUSE TO HIDE (Book #3)
CAUSE TO FEAR (Book #4)
CAUSE TO SAVE (Book #5)
CAUSE TO DREAD (Book #6)

KERI LOCKE MYSTERY SERIES
A TRACE OF DEATH (Book #1)
A TRACE OF MURDER (Book #2)
A TRACE OF VICE (Book #3)
A TRACE OF CRIME (Book #4)
A TRACE OF HOPE (Book #5)

CHAPTER ONE

Train doors swished shut behind her, and now she was alone. Amber's heels clicked against the grimy tiled floor as a couple of dim, buzzing fluorescent tube lights illuminated the train stop. It was late, so most of the station was empty.

As she moved forward, a small door opened along the wall, and she spotted a janitor pushing a yellow mop bucket around a beige column, water droplets sloshing onto the floor and stippling dark spots across the dusty ground. She smoothed the front of her blouse, frowning at the wrinkle near the second button that refused to submit.

She let out a faint sigh, brushing strands of frazzled hair behind an ear and making a beeline for the green exit sign at the base of the stairs. Exhaustion lingered along her limbs, weighing them down after a long day of work. Driving in Paris was simply impossible, but the train came with its own particular obstacles.

She listened to the faint whir of the fleeing locomotive on the tracks behind her. A faint breeze wafted past her, dabbing at her warm neck— the air current caused by the train jetting through the dark, underground tunnel only fifty yards to her right, near a compartment for lockers.

She winced suddenly, resisting the urge to slap her head. She needed to grab her daughter's weekend bag from the locker where she'd left it that morning. Her ex had agreed to pick Claire up from her friend's sleepover the next morning, and Amber had agreed to meet him halfway, dropping the bag off at his apartment. It was on the way, after all—at least, so she'd reasoned.

She sighed, her footsteps still clicking against the dusty tile as she rerouted and headed for the rain lockers. The buzzing lights cast her shadow past her, stretching it toward the edge of the platform as if the silhouette were peering down onto the tracks.

She heard a flutter of motion behind her, and her heart skipped. She shot a quick look back, her blonde hair swishing across her sweaty face. But it was just the janitor again, whistling as he locked a door to a closet and moved off in the other direction, leaving her alone.

She paused, standing in the sudden silence. The train was gone now. The janitor vanished. The sound of traffic from the streets above was little more than a dull hum. She'd never quite realized just how...

1

isolated these places could be so late at night. A faint shiver probed up her spine, like cold, trailing fingers.

She brushed hurriedly at her hair again, once more trying to smooth the annoying wrinkle on her shirt, and then—wincing where her palm caught against the second button—she continued toward the lockers.

As she moved into the three-sided room, lined with rectangular doors, she fished her keys from her pocket, pulling out the rental. She glanced at the number on the side, then stepped past the key disposal slot behind her and approached the locker.

As she pressed the teeth into the keyhole, though, something caught her eye.

She froze.

A faint trail of juice was spilling from the locker above her own, trailing down in sticky, viscous patterns where it eventually pooled on the floor in a slick sheen of crimson. Briefly, she caught her reflection in the puddle of red.

Amber inhaled faintly. She detected an odd, semi-sweet, coppery scent lingering on the air. She stared at the locker above her own. At first, all she could think was that some moron had stowed their lunch and forgotten it. If a juice box had ruined Claire's favorite jeans, Amber was going to be furious...

But something about the strands of red down the face of gray metal gave her pause. She reached out with shaking fingers, still holding her key.

It was then that she realized someone had left the top locker *open*. Just a crack. Enough that she glimpsed a faint slit of black up and down the side of the metal door.

The same prickle from earlier reintroduced itself to her spine. Almost despite her best instincts, she reached up with a shaking hand and gripped the handle to the locker above hers. She stood frozen for a moment, feeling the handle's cold metal against her skin. That tinny scent still lingered on the air.

"Hello?" she called quietly, glancing over her shoulder suddenly. But no response. She wasn't sure who she was even speaking to. The locker was far too small for a person... No sign of the janitor behind her. No other passengers on the platform.

She was alone and couldn't shake a rising sense of horror in her gut.

She twisted the handle to the locker, even though it was already unlocked, shivering as she did. As the door pulled open, she stared inside... and her eyes bugged.

2

The first thing she spotted was the cheap burner phone facing her. A white light blinked next to the camera, suggesting it was recording video. But just as quickly, her eyes darted down.

That's when she spotted the severed human finger.

Her mouth opened, and she let out a shaking exhale. Halfway through, it began to turn into a scream. But before she could fully release the astonished cry, the phone in the locker began to ring.

The blinking white light continued to pulse above the severed, bloody finger as a faint, playful ring-tone emanated from the locker. A ringtone with bells and flutes and faint humming. In fact, Amber thought she recognized it as a child's nursery song.

The phone continued to ring insistently as Amber stared into the locker. The light continued to blink as if watching her like some cyclops. She wanted to turn and scream... She needed to call the police. But her own phone was nearly dead.

And this one? Perhaps she could just use it.

Breathing through her mouth now in quick, shallow puffs, she summoned all her inner courage built over the course of nearly five years as a single mother. Her hand shot into the locker, snaring the phone and ripping it out. She must have bumped something on the cheap touchscreen, because a second later, a voice crackled from the speaker.

"H-hello?" the voice said, desperately, shaking with fear. A child's voice...

Suddenly, her eyes widened. "C-claire?" she whispered.

But no. Not her daughter. In fact, when the voice spoke again, she wasn't so certain it belonged to a child. More like someone play-acting. A sugary, innocent voice like from some cartoon. A caricature of a child's voice. This, along with the nursery rhyme ringtone, nearly made Amber drop the phone completely.

But the voice seemed to sense her hesitation. "P-please," it said. "I need your help. Please help me!"

She didn't reply. Didn't want to speak with the creepy voice on the phone. She refused to look in the direction of the finger now.

"P-please... I need help! Help me! Look, I'm in the train station. You have to let me out!"

At this, she stiffened. She'd been in the middle of hovering her thumb over the red button. She swallowed and said, "I can call the police!"

"No!" the voice said sharply. "Help me. I'm very close. *Very* close. Just—look behind the locker room. There's a hall. Can you find it?"

The voice still spoke in a sing-song, shaking, childish tone. But now, in the longer sentences, she detected the mistakes. An older voice—a male voice. A man. He was putting on some pretense. For what twisted reason, she didn't know. Already, she realized she'd stumbled into something horrible.

Right now, all she wanted to do was grab her daughter's overnight bag, call the cops, and run.

"Help!" the voice said.

On the other hand, what if he really *did* need help? But no… no, she refused. She hung up. She dialed the number for the police, waiting quietly. "Hello!" she said, once the ringtone stopped and she heard a breath. Before the operator could even reply, she was shouting, "I'm in the L'aderu train station! Please—send help. Someone's down here in trouble. I found a finger!"

She listened to a hurried response and repeated her details, but then her hand shook from the phone's vibration. Another incoming call from a blocked number. She stared at the device, allowing it to ring… ring…

Help…

What if she was wrong about the voice? What if someone was in trouble? She shot a look toward the finger, wincing. Then, feeling a bit better that the police were on their way, she reluctantly put the police on hold and answered the call again.

"Alright," she said hurriedly. "I'm behind the lockers. Where are you?"

She moved around the small, three-sided space. A small hall led behind another large, beige column. She spotted a supply closet. Not unlike the one the janitor had locked on the other side of the platform.

With quick footsteps, double-checking the police were still on the line, though on hold, she hastened toward the small doorway.

"Yes," the voice was saying. "Just down the hall. See the door? Let me out. I trapped myself in the closet. Please help me!"

"I… the police are coming," she said. "Can we wait?"

"I can't breathe!" the voice protested. It began to hyperventilate.

Amber gritted her teeth, trying to think clearly. But she felt disoriented from the long day, the exhaustion, the blinking light on the camera. She just wanted to get home.

So carefully, at arm's distance in case she had to make a break for it, she reached out, gripping the handle to the closet.

And that's when she spotted the blood. A puddle of red liquid spreading from under the door, across the tiles. She stared and slowly tugged the closet handle.

The hinges creaked as the door swung slowly open, revealing a janitorial supply closet.

And there, tucked beneath a row of cleaning supplies, under a wooden shelf, she spotted a body.

"Thank you," the voice on the other line said with a chuckle. "Thank you for helping…" And then the line went dead.

She just stared at the corpse, lifeless eyes gaping back at her. The dead woman's hand was missing a finger. Barely thinking, she put the police back on the line but couldn't bring herself to speak.

"Hello?" a voice was calling from the receiver. "Hello, ma'am, can you hear us?"

The corpse leered at her. But by opening the door, she'd allowed a broom to fall. The jarring motion dislodged one of the corpse's arms. And suddenly, the head slumped as if drifting off to sleep, long hair cascading toward a disheveled, flower-patterned dress.

This was too much for Amber.

She gulped air, gaped into the closet, and let out a shrill, ear-splitting scream.

CHAPTER TWO

"Keep your voice down," Adele insisted. "I'm fine, John. Really, I am." Agent Adele Sharp winced as she pushed from the couch in her apartment's living room and maneuvered around her boyfriend to try and approach the small half-fridge she'd installed weeks ago for the exclusive purpose of holding her father's stash of beer. The first rays of morning sunlight beamed through the window over the kitchen table, warming her skin.

Now, she used the fridge mostly for ice packs and pistachio ice cream. Either of them, in that moment, would have been better medicine than the small bottle of painkillers John was shaking beneath her nose.

Adele brushed past him, hiding her grimace of pain as best she could. She couldn't help her fingers instinctively fluttering to her ribs, though, testing the bandage beneath her simple, white cotton shirt.

"Be reasonable, American Princess!" John growled. "I'm trying to help. The doctor said—"

"I know what the doctor said!" Adele snapped. She moved right past the half-fridge, if only to escape proximity with that cursed pill bottle. Instead, she approached the window, pretending to adjust the blinds.

The pain in her side no longer lanced every time she moved. She could walk—even jog short distances without *too* much discomfort—as long as she didn't twist at the waist. It had been nearly two weeks since the intruder had broken into her apartment and stabbed her, leaving her for dead on her own apartment floor.

She'd managed to chase the bastard out, though.

But there was still neither hide nor hair of the home invader. No one had managed to find him. No cameras had spotted him. Agent Renee had personally been up and down the street she lived on, looking at every ounce of footage he could find. The DGSI had mobilized a unit to try and find the culprit.

But two weeks later, they hadn't made much progress.

Thankfully, the same couldn't be said for her wound. The killer had narrowly missed piercing anything vital. The pain remained, but the stitches, the bandages, the two weeks of repeated hospital visits had done their work. She could move again without gasping in pain.

At least that was *something.*

Agent Renee, though, wasn't nearly so impressed. "I see you in pain when you think I'm not looking," John insisted. "Just take half." He shook the bottle again. "Please."

But Adele kept her back to her partner, staring out the window onto the Parisian streets below, her eyes trailing over bus stops and wide sidewalks. "I don't need those things," she said. "They muddy my mind."

John let out a snort of exasperation. "And I don't suppose staying at the site of the attempted murder *also* is somehow compromising your ability as an investigator? Come on, Adele. Be reasonable."

She turned now, her eyes flashing. At five-foot-nine, Adele was taller than most women, and could generally meet the eyes of most men at an even level.

But Agent Renee was well over six foot. His handsome, sharp features were now twisted into a glower. A single Superman curl of dark hair angled down his forehead. A scar twisted up the side of his neck, teasing the base of his chin. She'd often likened him to a James Bond villain—usually in affectionate terms.

Now, though, he was just a nuisance.

"I'm fine here," she said. "I don't need those." She pointed to the painkillers. "And I already told Foucault I'm cleared for duty. Doc signed off on it."

John threw his hands up. "Foucault agreed? Is he insane?"

Adele just rolled her eyes, crossing her arms and holding back a wince. "As for my apartment," she said, "it's *mine.* I'm not going to let some random creep scare me away. Besides, he's not coming back."

"You don't know that!"

"No? That's what the officer standing outside my door is for, isn't it?" she retorted. If she looked beneath the door, she could just about make out the shadow of the police officer stationed outside.

It had been part of her deal with Foucault to get him off her back. He'd seemed intent on relocating her also, just like John. But Adele didn't need to move. Didn't want to move. This was *her* home, dammit. She rarely felt comfortable in any given place, and she wasn't about to give this one up so easily.

Granted, the home was starting to feel a *bit* like a prison. Sooner or later, she hoped Foucault would assign her a case. She'd been cleared for nearly a week now, though admittedly had exaggerated the progress of her healing.

But if there was one thing Adele Sharp hated more than knife wounds, it was lingering around her apartment with nothing to do except sulk.

She needed a case. She also needed Agent Renee to drop the damn issue.

Which, of course, meant he did the exact opposite.

"Fine," he said, slamming the bottle of pills on the table. "You won't take these. You won't move out. I'll sleep in my car on the street then. Is that what you want?"

"Suit yourself," Adele muttered. "Make sure you have a lot of leg room—I hear sleeping in cars can cause cramps."

The two of them glared at each other across the room, John's massive hand resting on the back of a cheap, wooden chair Adele had bought online and assembled herself. One of the screws was missing in the frame, but she'd found a piece of wire to jam into place instead. Perhaps she wasn't the *best* homemaker, but she'd never claimed to be anything besides an investigator.

And now, even that was on hold.

They still had no clue who the attacker had been. No clue *what* he'd wanted. He'd been wearing a ski mask. Had known to check her door hinges for tape, had known to avoid the cameras, had entered the building without being seen.

A professional? Or just an experienced pervert?

An acolyte of the Painter? This was what worried her most. She'd killed the serial killer who'd hunted her mother and Robert and her ex, and while she still dealt with the guilt of her choices, she hadn't considered there might be *others* who'd want to make her pay for what she'd done.

But the Painter had always taunted or played with his prey. The attacker in her apartment hadn't said a word. So if not the Painter, then what?

As much as she put a bold face on it, Adele had spent many sleepless nights running through the attack. The sudden sharp pain. The realization that someone was in the dark with her. Then the ensuing fight.

He'd gotten away, *barely*. She'd lived.

Also barely. Luckily, she'd had her phone to call for help.

It wasn't like she *blamed* John for his concern. In a way it was touching... in a somewhat overbearing, mildly obtrusive sort of way. He'd been pestering her for days now to move out of the apartment.

Whenever the subject came up, though, she could feel her temper rising. And today was no exception, evident by the faint knock on the door.

"Hello?" the officer in the hall called. "Everything alright?"

"We're fine!" John and Adele snapped at the same time.

The cop cleared his throat but went quiet, likely realizing he wasn't needed. Adele and John met each other's gaze, each of them like an iron bar, refusing to bend. Robert Henry, Adele's old mentor, had once used the phrase *iron sharpens iron*... But in Adele's experience, strong-willed people just pissed her off.

She inhaled shakily, forcing herself to calm. "I'm not going to abandoned this place, John. My mother used to…" She trailed off, biting back any further retort. She had no interest in opening this can of worms.

John, though, displayed no such aversion. "I *know* your mother and you used to live here," he said with a long sigh. He ran his calloused trigger finger through his dark hair, pushing the errant strand of bangs back into place. The moment his hand lifted, though, the tuft of hair fell promptly back over his eyes.

His gaze softened somewhat as he studied her. The hand in his hair moved to scratch at his scarred chin. Adele knew bits and pieces concerning his past. She knew he'd once served on French special forces, and that his last tour had ended poorly. People had died. John had survived. It haunted him still.

There was something similar to a haunted quality in his gaze as he watched her. He swallowed, his Adam's apple bouncing. Then he just gave a shrug of his broad shoulders. "Have it your way," he muttered. "Just… just take care of yourself, alright?"

Adele opened her mouth to reply, but before she could, her phone began to ring. A second later, John's also began to chirp.

Frowning, the two of them lifted the devices to their ears. Adele answered with a curt, "Yes?" She waited impatiently. "Mhmm," she said. "Alright. Now?"

John looked at her as he lowered his own phone. Adele clicked hers off a second later. "Work?" John said.

Adele nodded curtly.

John bit his lip. "So Foucault wants you on the case? You sure you're ready?"

Adele reached out, patting John on the arm. "I appreciate the concern, Renee. But I'm coming. We can drive together or separately. Your call."

He muttered darkly, but then fished his keys from his pocket, moving toward the door. Adele followed after him, grabbing her jacket and wallet from the counter by the door. She passed the bottle of painkillers on her kitchen table without a second glance.

CHAPTER THREE

The opaque door swung shut behind her as Adele entered Foucault's office. The place had grown familiar over the years. She slowly settled in a chair in front of the large oak desk. The scent of air fresheners no longer gave her a headache as it once did.

As she settled into the chair, she moved with very slow motions. Bending and rising exacerbated the pain in her side more than anything.

Agent Renee flopped into the chair next to her, flinging his large feet up onto the coffee table and crossing his legs and arms. He looked every bit a petulant child as he shot her angry glances, especially looking toward her side. Her hand hovered over the area of the wound just in case the bandage had started seeping. The last thing she needed was for Foucault to see blood.

She'd been itching for a case for weeks and wasn't about to let John's bad mood—even a bad mood on her behalf—ruin the opportunity.

Foucault eyed her over his oak table, one dark brow quirked. He had features like a bird of prey, with a hooked nose and a sharp chin. His lips pressed into a thin line and when he spoke, he did so with the rasp that accompanied a lifetime of chain-smoking.

"Moving slowly there, Sharp. Are you alright?"

She didn't hesitate. "Yes, sir. Absolutely fine."

John rolled his eyes. Adele ignored it.

Foucault folded his hands, elbows in his neat blue suit resting on the lacquered surface of his oversized table. "Right then," he said, "to business." He glanced between the two of them, both his eyebrows dropping now and forming a furry, dark angry caterpillar across his forehead. "Two victims so far. One of them in our backyard."

"Paris?" John said, leaning forward now.

"Yes, Renee. At a train station here. The other victim was at a train station in Hamburg."

"Germany and France?" Adele said, also perking up now. "What's the MO?"

"He…" Foucault nibbled a lip. "Ah… How do I say this delicately… The killer is leaving *parts* of his victims in lockers to be found. He then guides, by phone, the discoverer of said part to the bodies."

"Parts?" John grimaced.

Foucault nodded. "An ear was left in a depot office. A finger in a locker. Both the bodies were hidden elsewhere."

John lowered his feet from the coffee table now, frowning at their boss. Adele sat straight-backed, not so much as twitching.

"Suffice it to say," Foucault said, "both victims share an MO. A severed body part, both women, and both found with a cheap phone near the appendage, camera on, light blinking. The killer seems to enjoy guiding unsuspecting passengers to find the bodies he's hidden."

"A pervert then?" Adele asked.

John just snorted. "Definitely a pervert."

"There has been no sign of sexual assault," Foucault replied. "I'll let you comb through the coroner reports yourselves, though."

Adele said, "If he's calling them by phone, have we been able to track the numbers?"

"No—he's using disposable phones. In addition, when he speaks, we think he's using a voice scrambler. The first victim said an old man was on the line. The second said a child spoke to her."

John gave a visible shudder, but was already pushing to his feet.

Foucault, used to Agent Renee's lack of decorum, just sighed and leaned back. "Both bodies have been found in major train stations in major cities," he called out. "The transportation authority is breathing down my neck. We had three trains ground to a halt yesterday. We can't afford this to continue." He leaned in now, staring directly at Adele. "This office has been cast in somewhat of an unfavorable light in the news recently…"

She cringed, thinking of her shooting of the Painter.

"Whether or not we deserve such treatment," he said softly, "we have to tread lightly on this one. And give the media—and the politicians—a reason to leave the DGSI alone. Is that clear?"

"Crystal, sir," Adele said. She pushed to her feet, standing next to John.

Foucault gave a dismissive wave. "Files are on your phones. Good luck, Agents. The Paris station is still cordoned off. Start there." He watched Adele for a moment. In a quieter voice, he said, "Are you sure you're feeling alright, Agent Sharp?"

"Fine," she said stiffly, though rising from the chair had caused another lance of pain. "Just fine, sir. We'll start at the train station. Thank you."

And with that, before he could change his mind or John could lodge a complaint, she pushed through the opaque door and back out into the hall of the DGSI headquarters.

John joined her a second later, but as the two of them began to move, Foucault's voice rang out behind them. "Agent Sharp! A word if you please."

She hesitated, shooting John a quick, uncomfortable glance.

He shrugged. "No clue," he whispered.

She glared at him. "You didn't say anything?"

John crossed a finger over his heart. "Not a word," he said. "I didn't do this…"

She sighed, adjusting her sleeves, smoothing her shirt, and facing the door. It was *never* a good sign to be called *back* into the executive's office. Everyone knew that.

A call back meant there was something he wanted to discuss in private. Which meant she'd done something wrong.

As she summoned inner courage, she shot a quick look down at her shirt, making sure the bandages weren't bleeding through. John stepped back from the door with a gallant, sweeping gesture.

And Adele pushed back into the room, breathing slowly.

"Close the door, please, Agent Sharp," Foucault said, waving a hand and gesturing for her to rejoin him by the desk.

She sighed and slowly approached, feeling a flicker of unease as she padded across the carpet using slow motions. The door clicked shut behind her, and she waited until Renee's large shadow shifted across the glass and disappeared.

She scowled. She wouldn't put it above John to be standing directly *next* to the door in an effort to hear every word. He wasn't exactly a respecter of privacy, or DGSI property for that matter. Hell, he'd converted an old interrogation room in the basement into his own personal bachelor pad, complete with speakeasy.

Still, Adele kept her eyes forward.

As she approached Foucault's desk, feeling a jolt of nerves, a couple of things occurred to her. They still hadn't officially declared their relationship to the office. John and Adele were required to file paperwork if they started dating. But in the past, this had meant agents were no longer allowed to team on cases.

The last thing she wanted was to lose John as her partner and figure out chemistry with a new investigator.

But Foucault's frown was a bit more severe than it might have been if it was simply a conversation about a concealed office romance. "I— yes sir?" Adele said, coming to a halt, still standing in front of the desk.

She made a big show of standing straight, shoulders back, looking as at ease as she could manage, even though some of her stitches felt as if they might be straining. Her side ached, but she refused to show it.

Foucault was just watching her. His frown shifted now, and he glanced at the table. "I... there's no easy way to say this, Sharp."

Her stomach fell. This was not a very good start.

"But..." He looked up.

"You're not dying, are you?" she said, eyes wide.

He blinked. "Pardon?"

"Oh... what? No. Sorry—so sorry. I just—" She shook her head, feeling a lance of embarrassment. She felt a suspicious thought wondering if John had snuck painkillers into her coffee that morning. They always made her a bit loopy.

She inhaled shakily and steadied again. "Sorry, sir," she murmured. "You were saying?"

"The shooting of your mother's killer," Foucault said without missing a beat. "I'm afraid we're launching an internal investigation."

Adele had been expecting anything but this. She stared. "An... an internal..."

"Just a formality," he said quickly. "Obviously, we both know it was a clean shooting. I've read the report. You did a good job, Sharp. But as I've said, the DGSI has recently been involved in some... unfortunate headlines. And so we're trying to make sure we have our i's dotted and t's crossed in case anyone higher up comes calling. Do you understand?"

"Yes... yes sir. And what's going to be required of me?" Adele asked stiffly, her knees feeling very weak all of a sudden.

He waved away the comment. "An interview. With me. Would you like to do it now, or later? Everything will be on record, and Agent Paige will be sitting in."

Adele felt a nasty little flicker of suspicion. "Was this Agent Paige's idea, sir?"

He wrinkled his nose. "Sophie? What—no. This was my idea, Adele. Like I said, it's a formality. We can start this instant if you want. The initial round is just name and basic information. Any further interviews can wait until after the case."

She felt a lead weight in her stomach. "More than one interview, sir?"

He nodded, frowning at her. "Paid, of course. That's not a problem, is it?"

She let out a long breath. "No... no sir."

14

"I can take you off the case if you're worried about time management," he said curtly. "This is a priority. And... Adele," he added quickly, "solving this case—this current case—will go a long way in appeasing any itching ears. Anyone who might..." He swallowed faintly, touching his tongue against his lower lip and scowling. "...be interested in vying for my job."

This last comment eased some of the tension in Adele's gut. So this was a political play. Office politics. Someone was vying for Foucault's job and wanted to use Adele's shooting for leverage.

Foucault looked at Adele, flashing a smile. "I'm sure it will all work out. But I do require some of your time. So would you like me to take you off the case? Are you ready to speak for a few minutes preliminarily?"

"No—the case, I mean. But also the questions. I'm feeling a bit dizzy, sir. Maybe we could do this a bit later?"

He frowned. "Dizzy? Why? I was told your doctor cleared you."

Adele resisted the urge to bite her lip. She was being harassed from all angles. She wasn't proud of it, but she decided to use the one excuse that had paid dividends in high school PE on more than one occasion. "I apologize, sir, it's just... this time of month..." She raised her eyebrows allowing her boss to make the implications for her.

First asking him if he was terminally ill. Now talking about her period.

Today was not going to be a good day.

Foucault, though, seemed to get the inference. He blinked and quickly leaned back, coughing delicately and looking determinedly at his computer screen. "Ah, yes... yes, I see. Alright, then. After the case. If that works. Certainly. Certainly... Good luck, Adele. Now, if you don't mind... I have some work."

It was amazing how mention of menstruation could so quickly shift the burden of discomfort.

She let out a long, whooshing breath and hurried back out the door, grateful that this time Foucault didn't call after her. But as Adele hastened away, she couldn't help but feel as if her own burden was still lingering.

Any time someone looked into the Painter's shooting, it would raise red flags unless she was careful.

Unless she lied.

CHAPTER FOUR

Adele didn't mention Foucault's comments to John. And Renee hadn't asked, likely assuming it had to do with her injury. But the real reason for her visit to the office was slowly slipping to the back of her mind, now, as they moved through traffic. She gripped the arm rest as John turned slowly past the stop sign, taking a street off the main avenue that led to their designated location.

She shot a suspicious glance at Renee, who stared determinedly ahead. A traffic light ahead turned slowly from green to yellow.

John applied the brakes gently, gliding to a smooth stop as the light flicked to red.

"Alright, what the hell!" Adele demanded, slapping a hand against her armrest.

John sniffed. "Whatever do you mean?"

"Why are you driving like a grandma?"

John glanced at her, one dark eye glinting beneath a curved arch. "Hmm?" he said innocently.

"You're observing the speed limit," Adele snapped, raising a finger. "You didn't try to speed through that yellow! And you even let a pedestrian *through* the crosswalk. What are you doing, Renee?"

"I," he said testily, "am making sure you are comfortable. I didn't realize I'd earn the third degree for being considerate."

Adele glowered. She'd been afraid he would say something like this. The last thing she wanted was for Renee to treat her differently on a case. The idea of being treated with kid gloves on a job she had earned made her stomach twist.

"Well," she said, "don't. Do your normal thing."

He sniffed. "And what is my normal thing?"

"I dunno." Her hand fluttered in front of her face as if painting a picture. "Break speed limits. Scare pedestrians. Stain the asphalt with rubber. You know, *Renee* things."

"Renee things… Staining asphalt with—have you been watching those racing movies?"

Adele glared through the windshield as the light turned to green and John began to move again, still annoyingly slowly.

"It was a long few weeks," she muttered. "Don't judge me." She sighed, feeling a flicker of guilt at her gruff tone. John was just trying to help. He didn't deserve to be harangued for consideration. Besides, it wasn't Renee she was mad at. It was whatever scumbag had broken into her apartment. Part of her wanted it to just be a run of the mill creep. Someone like that wouldn't return. Not after she'd stationed a cop outside her door.

But what if it was something else? What if the Painter had friends?

Adele closed her eyes, trying to stave off the threat of a headache. She exhaled slowly, counting to five. And then, softer, she said, "Thank you for being considerate."

"You're welcome. There's a stop sign ahead. Mind if I slow, or should I take out that old man in the crosswalk—wait, no, I think that stroller might protect him."

Adele snorted, glancing at her partner. John's eyes twinkled mischievously. One of the things she liked most about Renee was the way the two of them rarely let hard words get between them. Both of them didn't think too highly of words. A lot of people talked. Few people did what they said.

John had risked his life for her on more than one occasion. She'd done the same in return.

She trusted him more than anyone in the world. Even if he was sometimes a sarcastic jackass. Though admittedly, she could be—in his words from the night before—a "stubborn blockhead." Not that she really knew what a *blockhead* was.

Words were words. Actions spoke louder. So did pictures.

Which was why she now fished her phone from her pocket and started to scroll. John shot her a look as he picked up the pace, following the GPS directions to the train station in Southern Paris.

Adele opened the file Foucault's office had sent to her encrypted email and began cycling through the report.

"Anything?" John said.

Adele felt a flash of relief that he'd turned attention to the case as well.

She paused, wrinkling her nose at a large, blown-up, glossy image of a severed finger. Below it, she spotted an ear, hardly cut with precision. Not a practiced hand, then.

"Maybe... robbery?" she murmured. "Obviously not *just* robbery..."

"What makes you say that?"

Adele turned the phone so John could see. "Tan ring around the finger. Missing ring. No one in the report mentions they found a ring."

John snorted, drumming his fingers against the plastic grip of his steering wheel. "You think this guy is going to these efforts just to steal some cheap ring?"

"We don't know it's cheap. And like I said, maybe he's veiling his real motives."

"We do know it's cheap," he said. "Look at the fingernail."

Adele did, then shrugged. "So what?"

"That's a cheap brand glue-on nail," he said with a nod. "Trust me, Bernadette used to send me to get them all the time."

Adele, who'd never tried glue-on nails in her life, just snorted. "Just because she had a cheap nail doesn't mean it was a cheap ring."

John shrugged. "Suit yourself. We won't rule out robbery. But it's got to be more than that, yeah? What else connects the victims?"

Adele scrolled back up the files once more, scanning quickly. She bit a lip, then murmured, "Both were women... but about a fifteen-year age difference. Different color hair. Different ethnicity. Different heights..."

"Were they both passengers?" John asked. He turned the steering wheel, following the GPS instructions to pull into a paid parking lot behind the entrance to the station. Ahead, at the top of the stairs, Adele spotted two stationed police officers by an orange sawhorse, blocking any entrance to that particular platform. The above-ground section of the station reminded her of a greenhouse, with large, slanted glass walls and many windows. She noted people moving about inside, stopping by the in-house coffee shops or picking up croissants from the bakeries as they went about their morning commutes.

The sun was higher in the sky now, reflecting off the many glass walls of the above-ground section of the large station. The parking lot alone was filled with vehicles—at least a couple hundred by Adele's hurried count. And this was only one of the lots used for commuters.

As John pulled into a parking spot, an attendant hurried over. John flashed his badge out the window, though, waving him away.

Adele, skimming the victims' files, clicked her tongue, finally discovering the answer to Renee's earlier question. "Yes," she said.

"What?"

"You asked if they were both commuters. Yes. Passengers both— neither worked for the train line."

John sighed. "Great. Mobile victims—that's always a fun twist."

Adele winced, slowly stowing her phone. She couldn't help but agree with Renee's sentiment. "The witness who found the finger was brought back here," she said quietly. "Probably shouldn't keep her waiting. She's had a long night."

John and Adele pushed out of their vehicle, emerging beneath the warm sunlight. She could feel Renee's eyes on her like a hawk's as she pushed into a standing position and let out a faint grunt. Her fingers fluttered to her ribs but dropped quickly. She covered by pretending she was checking the hem.

She met his gaze and gave an innocent shrug. "What?"

"I'm watching you, Sharp," he muttered. "I'm not going to let you kill yourself. Just so we're both clear. If I have to report you to Foucault myself…"

She snorted, shaking her head. "Never took you for a tattle-tale, John."

"Me neither," he snapped. "Call it personal growth."

"I'd rather call it annoying."

"Suit yourself!" He marched past her, leading the way toward the two officers by the sawhorse. With a quick nod of greeting and two raised identifications, John and Adele—still bickering—moved down the stairs into the dark, underground portion of the two-level Parisian train station, toward the crime scene and to go speak with the witness.

CHAPTER FIVE

Watching the passengers was like watching clothed birds... but bigger. The watcher smiled at this comparison, quickly pulling out his little brown notebook and scribbling down the simile... or was it a metaphor? He could never quite distinguish between the two.

He looked up again, still smiling as he so often did. There was a lot in life to be happy about. Maybe not for others. Certainly not for whoever his gaze landed on and settled... but for him? Life was just peachy.

Still smiling, he scanned the birds, his gaze searching for the one with the proper feathers. He'd always studied feathers—the various plumage, coloring, and texture. Of course, the feathers *he* looked for were of a more concrete variety.

He glanced up from his notepad, jotting down another observation, his gaze sweeping the rattling train compartment as they crossed a jarring portion of rail. The man with the newspaper across from him grimaced, folding his source of entertainment.

The woman next to him swaddled her child, cooing at him while trying to keep her voice down. He scanned their fingers. Their ears. Their necks. Searching... searching... He had an eye for detail. It was one of the reasons he'd been so fond of *her.*

She had enjoyed how he'd been able to pay attention to the little things. Next to his notebook, on his lap, he carried a burner phone which he'd purchased not far from the train station. He liked picking these up *right* before he needed them. Less time to have any inconvenient attention...

Now, surreptitiously, still smiling, he cycled to the camera. Hiding the device behind his journal, he raised the camera, taking pictures of the birds.

He pushed to his feet, moving slowly down the aisle, rocking and swaying with the motion of the train. As he moved, he took more pictures. Every so often, he stopped and stooped inside an alcove, near a rail or by an empty seat. He would then scroll through the pictures, his finger grazing the smooth glass.

He made a pinching motion with his fingers, zooming in on a picture of the woman in the green seat. He frowned at her fingers... No.

No, he'd been mistaken.

He hissed in frustration, cycling to the next photo of the fresh-faced beauty with the long legs. In a way she almost reminded him of his once-lover. He froze, staring at her hand... That was it. He recognized it.

He let out a shuddering little breath, his eyes widening. An announcer's voice was blaring over the speakers, declaring the names of the upcoming stops. But all he could do was stare at the pretty thing, her legs crossed so primly, her head dipped into the pages of some novel with a pink cover. He smiled as he stared at her.

One hand now gripped the green bar at his side for stability, still swaying and rocking on his feet. He continued watching her, his eyes bright, attentive, taking in every contour, feature, and detail. Yes... yes, *this* was the next one.

She looked up suddenly, lowering her book briefly. Her eyes met his. He smiled congenially.

"Creep," she muttered, ducking her head again and hunching her shoulders.

The accusation didn't bother him. *She* had said worse things all those years ago, after all. The train slowly came to a screeching stop. Passengers brushed past him in their haste for the exits. He just stood, watching the young woman, making no qualms about it.

"Hey, man," someone snapped at his side. "Leave the lady alone."

He glanced up and over. An old gentleman with a white beard and newsboy cap was glaring at him.

The watcher studied the newcomer, flashing another smile.

"Wipe that grin off your face," the old man snapped. "You've been eyeballing the young lady since the last stop. You should get off here..." It didn't sound like a request.

The watcher just shrugged. He reached out, patting the old man on his shoulder. The accuser stiffened as the watcher slipped by. He kept staring at the girl, even as he disembarked. He watched the way she let out a faint huff of relief and turned to thank the old man once he'd left the train onto the platform.

What neither of them saw, of course, was the way he hurried two doors down and boarded again—the very same train. One hand stowed his small journal. The other touched at the items in his pocket. Another phone—similar to the first. And his favorite knife.

He couldn't help himself. He smiled again, two compartments down from where his target still read her stupid pink book. Her superhero with his stupid flat cap got off at the next exit.

No more protectors now.

He watched through the passengers, eyes never leaving her, waiting as the train continued. He would have waited for hours, for years…

Luckily, he didn't have to.

The young woman jerked up at the voice announcing over the intercom. She quickly closed her book, unfolded those long, smooth legs of hers, and hastened toward the exit.

He watched through the window as she disembarked.

And then he followed.

CHAPTER SIX

Adele noted the way her footsteps almost created an echo in the nearly empty underground platform. The high ceiling flickered with long tube bulbs. A row of lockers was visible around the edge of a three-walled segment near one of the tunnels. Police stood by the lockers, while a forensics team picked through the crime scene.

Further away, behind a support column, as if intending to hide the view of the lockers, a woman was sitting in a plastic folding chair, sipping on something warm. A female police officer sat next to her, occasionally murmuring some soothing comment or jotting something down on a notepad.

"Our witness," John grunted at her side, nodding toward the woman behind the pillar.

Adele hesitated briefly, taking a couple of steps to the right to scan the crime scene itself. She spotted the same locker that had been in the high-definition, glossy crime scene photos provided by Foucault. She also noted streaks of red down the front of the unit. Behind the three-sided partition, more officers were moving through a small, cramped hall.

"Body was found back there," Adele said, pointing.

"Finger there." John nodded at the lockers. "Body there." He glanced down the hall. "Why separate them if he's going to keep them so close together?"

"A message?" Adele said. She bit her lip. "Think you could speak to forensics?"

John glanced at her. "You want to talk to the witness alone?"

"She's scared," Adele said. "And you have something of an intimidating presence."

John grunted, already turning to stalk away toward the crime scene. "Intimidating presence," he muttered as he left.

Adele watched the tall man leave, noticing he was already attracting attention from the other law enforcement officers, and then she turned, moving hastily toward the victim in the folding chair. As she drew nearer, she heard the female officer saying, "DGSI is almost here. I'm sorry, Ms. Lorenz—it shouldn't be much…" The policewoman paused, regarding Adele as she drew nearer.

A flash of Adele's identification received a quick nod. The officer made to rise from her seat, as if to offer it, but Adele just held out a hand and gave a quick shake of her head.

The woman in the folding chair glanced between the two of them nervously. "C-can I go now?" she asked. "I've told you everything I know."

Adele studied the woman with a quick once-over. Amber Lorenz, according to the initial report, had been traveling late the previous night; more accurately, *early* this morning. She'd been the one to find the body. And she looked like it. Every bit as flustered and frazzled as Adele might have expected.

"Apologies, Ms. Lorenz," Adele said softly. "My name is Adele Sharp, and I'm with the DGSI. Do you mind if I ask you a couple more questions? The moment we finish, I'll ask this nice officer to drive you home."

The policewoman flashed an encouraging smile, nodding at the witness. Behind them, Adele could hear the mutter of voices as police navigated the crime scene.

She focused her attention on their witness. "I'm told you got off the train at half past midnight."

Ms. Lorenz let out a shaking sigh as if resigning herself to the inevitable. She gave a brief shake of her head, her short hair moving less than it might normally have when not sweaty and unkempt. Ms. Lorenz had pleasant features, round cheeks and eyes with far more wrinkles than someone her age should have carried.

"It was closer to one," Lorenz said softly. "The train was running late."

"And is that when you found the body?"

"Umm... not at first. No. I went to get an overnight bag for my daughter."

Adele made to turn, glancing past the large column toward the three-sided partition by the tunnel wall. "And that's when you found the finger?"

"Y-yes," Ms. Lorenz said, biting her lip, her voice as shaky as her trembling hands. She clasped her palms together, folding them in her lap if only to hold them still. She swallowed and added, in a small voice, "It was so... shocking. I didn't even know what it was at first." She sobbed, but inhaled a shaky, steadying breath and pressed on. "But it was the camera that I noticed first."

"The phone?"

"Yes. It was facing toward me. And then... then it began to ring."

"The voice," Adele continued, her tone low, soothing, "what did it sound like?"

"At first… at first I thought it was a child… But the police say—" She glanced at the officer in the second chair. The woman nodded sympathetically and looked up at Adele, some of her neat brown hair tucked back in a bun falling out of place, over an eye. She huffed a breath, lifting the fallen bangs and hastily stowing them back in her scrunchy as she said, "We believe he's using a voice scrambler. Probably something he downloaded online."

"Tech working on it?"

She nodded.

Adele nodded. The woman's report matched what she'd read in the file. Which was to say, there wasn't much to go on. Now, she glanced back at the officer.

"Do you still have the phone?"

She nodded, waving past the column toward forensics. "Yes, ma'am. But we couldn't track it."

"I know," Adele said. "Saw that. But I was wondering more about—"

"No serial number either. He burnt it with acid."

Adele huffed, nodding again, glancing back at the witness. Her stomach twisted and turned, and she winced as she shifted her weight, her hand darting instinctively to her ribs. Down here, alone, late at night, she couldn't help but imagine the woman's fear when finding the finger. Then the creepy voice over the phone leading her to the rest of the body in the closet.

The killer was clearly trying to make an impression. A run-of-the-mill sadist? Or something else?

She shook her head… Why sever the finger? Just to add to the ghastly spectacle, or an intentional attempt to befog the crime scene?

She glanced back at their witness. "Anything else you can think of? Did you see anyone down here?"

The woman hesitated, glancing off in the opposite direction for a moment as if envisioning something. But then she seemed to think better of it. "No one was here… I mean, the janitor but he was leaving."

Adele gave an encouraging smile. "No one by the lockers? No one in the hall? Did you see anyone watching you?"

Each question was rewarded with a nibbled lip and a quick shake of the head.

Adele found her frustration mounting, but she kept it in check. There was no reason to make this woman feel worse. She glanced around the station now. The killer had burned the serial number of the burner phone. He hadn't stuck around to be seen. He was cautious, careful. There simply wasn't much to go off from the witness testimony.

It made sense, in a way. The killer had *wanted* his murder discovered by this woman. Which meant he would have taken great pains to avoid her finding anything he *didn't* want her to know.

She needed a better witness. A less tired, less scared witness.

Her eyes flitted up, scanning the ceiling. Two spots where she glimpsed round, domed lenses blinking down at her.

Cameras.

It was worth a shot.

Adele flashed another quick smile at the witness, hoping it was received as reassuring rather than queasy. "Thank you," she said quickly. "I appreciate your time." She glanced at the golden name tag of the accompanying officer. "Officer Francois will take you home." She said it lightly with a quirk of an eyebrow, simultaneously offering and requesting to the two listeners. The policewoman nodded once, and Ms. Lorenz melted in her chair, emitting a long sigh of relief.

Adele gave a quick nod of gratitude, but as she turned, she paused, frowning. "Excuse me—quickly, is the station manager down here?"

Officer Francois hesitated as she rose from her seat. But then she nodded quickly, pointing toward a man standing by the edge of the platform and speaking animatedly with, of all people, Agent Renee.

"Thanks," Adele said. Then she turned curtly and marched back in the direction of her partner. Before she drew close, she hesitated, pausing long enough to gather her breath, to allow the tightness in her ribs to recede again. Once she was sure her stitches weren't ready to split, she picked up the pace again, glancing every so often to the ceiling, searching out the cameras.

Two—no, three. Three eyes in the sky.

If anyone would be a reliable witness, it was these glassy black domes.

CHAPTER SEVEN

As she approached Agent Renee and the station manager, she caught a bit of their conversation. Given John's personality and the manager's posture, she wasn't stunned to detect a note of acid.

"I've been doing this for fifteen years, *young* man!" the manager exclaimed, his voice like a whip. "What exactly are you implying?"

John paused. Most people would have considered words to defuse the situation. John, though, blunt as ever, answered the question directly. "Incompetence," he said simply. "How is it possible that two of your cameras aren't working?"

Adele winced at these words, approaching now.

"Not two! Not two!" the manager exclaimed, waving a finger beneath Renee's nose like a conductor's wand. "Just one. That one." The finger now jammed skyward to a camera facing the stairs. "Last week someone threw a rock at it."

Adele leaned in, clearing her throat as she neared. Both men turned to look at her, wearing matching glowers. She held up her hands as if surrendering. "Don't shoot," she said. "I come in peace."

She took a moment to acknowledge the manager. He rocked on his heels, his back to the train tracks with an ease and indifference born of familiarity. Adele, on the other hand, was always uncomfortable near train tracks. As a child, she'd once been told that stepping on the metal would electrocute her. To this day, she wasn't sure if her mother had just been lying to try and keep her safe.

She wasn't about to test the theory.

Instead, she returned her attention to the manager himself. He wore a bright crimson tie tucked inside a green V-neck sweater. His arms were crossed, the baggy sleeves half rolled up his forearms. His eyes narrowed as he surveyed the two of them, his gaze whipping back and forth in anger.

"Is this your ape?" he asked Adele, pointing to John.

Renee flashed his teeth as if about to bite the waving finger.

Adele interjected quickly, "You know what they say. Don't touch the animals." Cautiously, she stepped between the two men. "As luck would have it, sir, I also want to know about the cameras. You are the manager, yes?"

"Gerard Barras!" he snapped as if it were an obvious answer she ought to have inferred from the ether. "I run this station and six like it. And until today, I haven't had any *murders*. Not until *you* showed up."

Adele sighed. "We show up after the murders, Mr. Barras."

"And who exactly are you?"

"DGSI," she replied.

"Never heard of it."

She frowned. "You are… French?"

He shrugged.

She sighed. DGSI had only been in operation for the last fifteen or so years. The federal bigwigs were still doing their best to establish their bona fides. Even the building they worked from was a newer acquisition.

She said, "Be that as it may, what do you mean your cameras aren't working?"

"Not *cameras*," he snapped. "Camera! Like I told the ape—"

"Careful," John growled.

The manager continued as if he hadn't been interrupted, "Only the one. And only because a vandal hit it last week."

"A vandal?" Adele said quickly. "What type of vandal?"

John shot her a look, his eyebrows inching up as he seemed to realize what she was getting at. It seemed, in Adele's estimate, mighty coincidental that a camera had been broken a week before the attack.

"We don't know," Barras continued with a sniff, adjusting the sleeves of his V-neck sweater. "He stayed on the stairs, out of the line of sight. Then the image cracked."

"What about those other two?" she said.

He glanced up, following her pointed finger. "Yes—they're working. That one faces the rails, though."

"And that one? The one near the lockers?"

He followed her gaze and sighed. "I—I… do you have a warrant?"

"Sir," Adele pressed, "is there a reason you don't want us to see the footage?"

"No!" he exclaimed. "No, of course not. Happy to help the GDI."

"DGSI."

"Whatever. Do you have a warrant? A judge's order?"

"No sir. We're in an active crime scene, investigating. We may have to extend that investigation to these other six stations you manage if we can't expedite this," Adele spoke smoothly. Normally she wouldn't have leaned so heavily in her first salvo. But he *had* called her boyfriend an ape, twice, in her presence. And while she knew John's

28

feelings were too underdeveloped to possibly get hurt, she took pride in being the only one allowed to tease him.

The manager's face fell. He muttered a couple of times but then sighed. "When do you need it by?"

"Five minutes ago," John growled.

Mr. Barras's cheeks were as red as his tie. He glanced past Renee toward the other police in the crime scene, and up the hall by the closet as if looking for a manager of his own to speak to. But when no one caught his eye, or even so much as glanced in his direction, he gave a deflated little sigh and held up the same waving finger. "One moment," he muttered. He gave a sniff, adjusted his tie, and marched off along the edge of the tracks toward a small office space.

Adele watched him retreat, then looked to John. "Making friends?"

He glared. "I blame my *intimidating presence.*"

Adele snorted. "Anything over there?"

He shook his head, glancing toward the hall. "Body was moved already. Forensics is dusting everything. Just cleaning products. Blood was cleared too."

Adele sighed. "Lockers?"

"Nada. What about the witness?"

"She's scared. That's about it. Killer used a voice scrambler. Seemed to get off on frightening her."

"Yeah—sounds about right. Sicko."

Adele didn't dispute this assessment. She and Renee both turned at the sound of quick footsteps. The short man in the crimson tie was huffing and puffing as he marched back in their direction, carrying a large tablet screen with an orange case. His combover lifted with each hurried motion. The short walk from the office seemed to have winded the man, and a faint stain of sweat was already forming under his neck along the edge of his undershirt collar.

Adele watched as Mr. Barras stopped, jamming the tablet toward her as if it were a tray of prison food. "There," he snapped. "First video was of the broken camera. Nothing to see—like I said. Second video from last night. Hours of footage. There's nothing. We already have been over it internally. Three times."

Adele nodded, impressed. "You guys move fast."

He glared at her. "Can we open the station again any time soon? We're going to miss morning traffic. We need both lines going to—"

John cut him off by snatching the tablet from his hands and turning it so Adele could see. The two of them leaned in, peering at the device. The first image was of a crowded underground station. Scores if not hundreds of people moved up and down the stairs, hastening through the terminal.

A few seconds passed, and then Adele spotted a quick motion and then the image went fuzzy. She looked at John. "Go back."

"What's the magic word?" he muttered.

"Hurry."

John smirked but hid it as he swiped his finger back a few seconds. He slowed the speed and the two of them watched closely. Foot traffic moved in and out of the station. Nothing happened at first. Then something large obscured the camera.

"What is that?" John asked.

Adele frowned. "Rock," she said.

The manager huffed. "Yes, yes—the vandal threw a rock. We found it after. But there's nothing to see—like I said!"

John shrugged, but Adele reached out, swiping back again. This time, she slowed the footage even further. Again, the rock appeared. She quickly tapped the pause button. "There!" she said, pointing.

John, and even the manager now, leaned in, staring.

It was barely a blur of black. But a figure was standing on the bottom of the steps. The footage was grainy and obscured. But Adele pointed. "His hand—see it?"

"I see pixels," John said.

"It's the little dot of white against the black outfit."

John turned his head one way, then the other. "You're sure that's not just more fuzz?"

Adele sighed. "It moved when the rock did. It's a hand. He flung a stone."

"What's that squiggle?"

"His hood. He's wearing a hood."

"Why's his face half hidden—"

"Sunglasses, John. Keep up."

John turned the tablet upside down. "Ah!" the handsome agent declared. "I see it now."

Adele rolled her eyes. "Good thing you pretty," she said.

"I get by on my looks," Renee agreed. "You, on the other hand, are brilliant enough to discover a squiggle with sunglasses and a pixel of white. By God, I think we've got him."

Now it was Adele's turn to glare. "I'm not saying we *got* anything. Clearly he knew the camera was there. But that's him."

"At least that's our vandal," John said.

"What are the chances that a rando takes out a camera before a murder?"

John hesitated, but shrugged. "Fine... I mean, I guess we can screenshot that pixel and see if the folk back at HQ can clean it up at all."

"No luck," the manager muttered. "We've tried. *With* a private agency," he added defensively.

But Adele just said, "It's worth a shot. Sir, we need you to send this file to us. I'll give you an email before I leave."

He didn't protest. Now, if anything, he seemed resigned to the inconvenience and just wanted to get it over with as soon as possible.

Adele swiped her finger along the smooth glass, shifting the image to the second video. This one provided a bird's-eye view of the station. She glanced at the timestamp in the corner. The footage rolled only a few hours before the body was found. She and John both watched closely. More commuters moved about in the grainy image. Hundreds of them going about their days, usually coming in flocks and then disappearing completely like spurts of water. Whenever a train arrived, the crowd would swell, when it departed it would diminish.

At about the 10 p.m. mark, as they sped at 8X through the video, Adele spotted something. "There!" she said. She hit pause.

This time, John spotted it. "Ah—there's our pixel again."

A man with dark glasses and a low hat, hands in the pockets of a thick, obscuring coat, was moving toward the edge of the platform.

He moved his head on a swivel, in just such a way to avoid being spotted. As he did, he flashed the bird toward the camera. At first, Adele thought he was flashing the middle finger, but a second later, as she leaned in, squinting, she realized it was the ring finger.

The same finger he'd severed on his victim. His head was still down, features obscured. The only thing that stood out was his flashing finger toward the camera as he moved out of sight, past the column behind which Adele had just been speaking with the witness.

Her skin prickled as she watched the image. John rewound. They watched again. Neither of them spoke, both desperately searching for clues. For *anything* that might stand out.

Adele's eyes bounced from the pixelated overcoat to the dark shoes. Everything generic. No visible name brands. No cartoons—no graphics. The killer's face completely obscured. They watched a third time as he flashed his finger once more.

"He's taunting us," John growled. "He knows what he's about to do. He knew we'd watch the camera. He's taunting..."

Adele didn't disagree. Her heart pounded as she stared at the small figure, disappearing off the edge of the screen to once more join a throng of pedestrians hastening in the other direction.

As she stared, she let out a long huffing sigh.

Not only was he taunting them, but he was smart. He'd broken one camera, then avoided the others. Worse still… Adele felt a jolt of fear.

John must have noticed something in her face, because he glanced at her and murmured, "What is it?"

She nodded at the figure on the screen. "He's establishing a relationship."

John paused, but then his jaw clicked as his teeth tightened. "Right. He wants us to know he's in charge."

"Not just that. He wants us to know this is just the start. This is his second victim. But if he's taunting cops, he's only growing more confident. He's not done yet. Not by a long shot."

These dark words lingered as John and Adele slowly lifted their gazes from the footage. Adele's throat felt like cotton. She swallowed, trying to focus once more. "We need that footage too," she said slowly, watching the station manager.

He was no longer protesting. He just nodded curtly. Then, in an eager tone, he said, "Is that all? Are you done?"

Adele paused, beginning to nod, but then catching herself.

"Actually," she said, "I have one last question." She held up a finger to match the manager's gesticulations. "The killer knew about the cameras. Had access to the lockers. Knew what route to take to obscure his features…"

"And?" the man insisted.

"And," John cut in, "we're wondering who might have access to that information."

He blinked for a moment, swallowing, the crimson knot of his tie bobbing. Suddenly, his eyes widened in realization. "W-wait… You don't think *I*—"

"Yes. You," John said.

At the same time, Adele said, "No—we're not accusing you of anything." She shot John a glare. He shrugged innocently. She continued, "But do you have any problem employees? Anyone who might know where to hide a body, the combinations for the lockers and locations of the cameras?"

The manager still looked flustered but was now clearing his throat, paying more attention to Adele than John like a parched man choosing between a cactus and an oasis. He said, "I—no one. No. I hire our employees personally. Some of the train lines that come through might

32

be worth investigating. But everyone who works at the station is personally…" He trailed off suddenly, hesitating for a moment. He tried to continue, to cover, but John snapped a finger.

"That name," Renee said. "The one you just thought of. Who?"

Adele watched silently.

"I—no one. No… no, no one. It's nothing."

Adele murmured. "Sir, this is a murder investigation."

He ran a hand through his combover. "I'm sure it's nothing," he declared. "But… well, we recently had to place one of our janitors on leave for comments made to a female tourist." He spoke this quickly, like someone ripping off a Band-Aid. "I must insist," he continued, "this is very out of the ordinary for me. The people I hire are reputable, reliable, and—"

"Janitor's name?" John cut in.

The man sighed, massaging the bridge of his nose. "I wouldn't even bring it up. Harassing comments and problematic social media posts are one thing… murder? No—not John."

Renee blinked. "The problem employee's name is John?"

The manager frowned. "Yes…"

"Yes!" Adele exclaimed. She caught herself though and coughed. "Umm, I mean—thank you, sir. For your cooperation. Last name? And you mentioned something about media posts?"

"Yes. John Gastone. He was hired a few months ago but let go. It wasn't just harassment. There were also… how do I say this delicately… inappropriately aimed photographs of some of our female commuters." The manager's cheeks were now beet red and he looked ready to hide behind a support column.

"Creepshots," John said.

"What?"

"That's what they're called online. Creepshots. Pictures of women without them knowing. Down their blouses or up their skirts or—"

"We get the picture!" Adele interrupted. "And also *yuck.*"

The manager looked ready to faint. Before he could protest further on behalf of his station's reputation or job performance, though, Adele said, "Is there anything else? You mentioned you wouldn't have brought up Mr. Gastone if not for something… Do you mean the pictures?"

"Those…" Another swallow and twist of the red tie. "But also he threatened violence against me when I let him go. Told me… told me he'd push me on the tracks."

John nodded as if he saw the reasoning behind the suggestion.

The manager took a step away from the edge, wincing uncomfortably. "I can provide you his address if you want. As he's no longer an employee here, I don't see the harm."

Adele was quick to nod. This time, John didn't interrupt. As the manager sighed, took his tablet, and began to move back to the office to retrieve the address, Adele turned away once more, staring down the hall where the body had been found. Her eyes skipped to the lockers again.

Why hide the finger in a separate location? What was the killer after? Why take the finger at all? He was taunting, toying with them. But something else motivated the mutilation.

She just had to figure out what.

CHAPTER EIGHT

Adele held her tongue as John drove like a geriatric once more, slowly maneuvering through the streets. She did her best to look chipper, energetic. Any time her side throbbed, she hid it. But John was onto her. He kept below the speed limit, guiding their car up the small road outside the old-fashioned brickwork apartments. The buildings were like one giant row of concrete. Each sewn into the other along the perfectly oriented, angled street lined with bus stops and sidewalks twice as wide as most of the ones found in either Germany or the US.

The GPS chirped as John pulled into an emergency parking spot outside Mr. Gastone's address. Adele slipped from the vehicle first, taking the sidewalk and hastening toward the front door of the apartment. The car door slammed behind her as John hastened to catch up.

Thanks to his long gait, John caught up quick enough until the two of them—side by side—were taking the steps to the front door.

As they reached it, Adele peered through the glass, plastered with notes for the apartment residents, searching for any sign of—

John ran his fingers down all the buttons.

Adele sighed. John darted in, stealing a kiss on her cheek. Then he straightened again, beaming as if he'd just won a prize. A second later, the door buzzed and John opened it with a gallant swing of his arm.

"After you, m'lady," he exclaimed.

Adele couldn't resist a smile. She tried to hide it, but it was nearly impossible to stay in a bad mood around Renee. Well... perhaps that wasn't true. Renee was almost always in a bad mood. But he was also always up to something. The combination of his grumpiness and his good humor made it difficult to take offense at anything he did, because it rarely felt like he much meant it.

The two of them took the stairs hastily, moving up the landings and hastening toward the second floor where Mr. Gastone's thick metal door met them at the end of the smoke-stained hall. Adele held her breath as she passed a no smoking sign, waving a hand in front of her face. A few trails of ash lingered on the air, suggesting someone had only just finished a smoke break.

They reached the door marked 208. John allowed Adele to stand on the opposite side of the door. Once her back was situated against the peeling flower wallpaper, her feet sturdy on the stained, brown carpet, Renee rapped his knuckles against the steel frame.

"DGSI!" he called. "Open up!" Then, clearly in a helpful mood, he added, "Police in case you don't know what that is!"

They received no reply. John knocked again, the staccato sound of thick knuckles against steel reverberating in Adele's ears.

Still no reply.

Adele frowned, pressing her cheek to the door, listening for any sound from the apartment within. No sounds were forthcoming. She shrugged at Renee.

He tried a third time…

"Shit," John said. "Hiding?"

She shrugged. "Hunting?"

They both wrinkled their noses. Adele heard a sudden rattle and glanced back to find the door next to the no smoking sign was opening. An old lady with more wrinkles than a pug peered out. Adele shook her head, flashing her badge and waving the woman back inside.

The lady sighed but swung her door shut with a faint *click.*

Adele returned her attention to the steel door. John tried the handle.

"Locked," he said.

"Thanks, Sherlock."

"Words hurt," he replied.

"Not you, they don't. Your skin is too thick."

He chuckled wickedly. "Not the only thick part of me."

"Renee… Did you try the bell?"

John shrugged, pressed the bell. A faint ringing sound reverberated from the unit. But still no movement. "I could call for a breaching team," John said. "Or we could look for the landlord. Or we could… or that."

Adele had dropped to a knee and tugged at the bristling mat in front of the door with tasteful, cursive scrawl that read *Welcome to Hell* instead of *Welcome Home.* As the mat pulled away, there was a faint scraping sound. She turned the mat over and pulled a key taped to the bottom.

John reached down, took the key, and inserted it into the lock as Adele returned to her feet, rubbing her hand off on her trousers in order to dislodge the faint sense of uncleanliness from rubbing against the stained floor which boasted all shades of *ick.*

The key slipped into the lock, and Agent Renee opened the door slowly. Adele's hand rested on her holster, her throat tense, eyes

36

searching for any sign of threat.

But the apartment was dark. No motion. No movement.

The faint stench of cigarette smoke in the hall competed with the much more potent version emanating from inside the unit. But while the space smelled like Foucault's office from two years ago, Adele's attention diverted to the images plastered across the walls.

Half-naked pictures of women with celebrity faces glued to voluptuous, silicone-injected bodies. John and Adele took hesitant steps into the unit, glancing around. More pictures lined the walls on the side of the hall. These didn't look like celebrities, but rather were full-blown prints of more candid shots.

"Well," Adele said softly. "Guy is definitely a creep."

John was moving down the hall, his gun now aiming at the floor. "DGSI!" he called, louder. He shouldered roughly through a door, then another. Adele followed behind him, her own weapon still holstered, but her hand lingering against it.

After a quick search of a bathroom and bedroom—with far worse pictures plastered above the headboard—Renee determined the coast was clear. Adele rejoined him in the room serving as a shrine for all things flesh.

John didn't quite seem to know where to look, so he settled on staring pointedly at Adele, tugging uneasily at his shirt. "Nice place," he muttered. "Think our little perv got another job?"

Adele tried not to choke on the smoky air. "Not sure… Doesn't look like the job holding type very much."

John snorted. "You can say that again."

The two of them both cast glances behind the couch and into the attached kitchen. But no movement. No sign of anyone. Mr. Gastone wasn't home.

Adele forced her way past John, back into the hall which had taken it easier on her sinuses. She pulled her phone from her pocket as John's voice echoed behind her, calling for a unit to come watch the apartment. For her part, she cycled to the information the station manager had provided.

Specifically, locating the social media profile. Mr. Gastone had been particularly active on his accounts, which was one of the reasons he'd been fired. She clicked to one of his forums, glancing at the most recent date. He hadn't posted anything in three days. She cycled back to the rest of the notepad document and clicked on a link for photo and video sharing.

And then she went stiff.

"John!" she called over her shoulder.

Agent Renee finished his own call and hurried into the hall, responding to the urgency in her tone. "Find something?"

She nodded, turning her phone so he could see. Adele then raised the volume, allowing the live-streaming audio to fill the hall.

"... a second body," Mr. Gastone's voice was saying, chuckling. "Right here in Hamburg. What are the odds, am I right? Well—G-strings, nice to have you all with me. But I'm gonna have to cut this short. My train leaves in an hour..." Adele and John stared as small emojis and little hearts swarmed up from the bottom of the image, and lines of text scrolled by in a chat box off to the side of the screen.

"He's live-streaming," John said.

"What's that?"

"He's streaming live."

"Oh." Adele frowned, staring at the image. "You heard him, right? He's in Hamburg."

"At our second crime scene, no less," John muttered. He trailed off as the video continued.

Mr. Gastone was saying, "I heard this lady was really pretty. Like *really* pretty. Man... ha! Wish I'd had a chance to see the body first. If you know what I mean." He let out a baying little chuckle. His face flashed into view once more. As he stared down at the camera, breathing heavily and giggling at his own joke, Adele stared at the ex-janitor's face. She didn't recognize him. Didn't know if he was the one who'd thrown the stone or avoided the cameras.

He had a pencil-thin, brown mustache. And judging by the parked cars he was strolling past, while breathing heavily, he wasn't very tall. Likely shorter than her. Mr. Gastone wore slick hair and had a cigarette tucked behind one ear. He continued prattling into the camera as more emojis and text scrolled by in the adjacent window.

"Anyway, G-strings," Gastone exclaimed, "I'm heading back to Paris now. Train's about to leave. I'll turn the stream back on if I find any merchandise I want to speculate on."

This comment received a bunch of smiley faces in the chat box. A couple of comments read *Perverts* or *weird stream...*

But mostly, the viewers—some five hundred—seemed to be enjoying the show. Whatever, exactly, the show was.

Judging by the images on Gastone's wall, and the behavior of some of the viewers, Adele wasn't particularly interested in finding out too much. She kept the stream open, though, until their suspect shut off his camera. Then the image went black.

Adele lowered her phone, frowning. "He was in Hamburg."

"That was the first victim, though," John pointed out. "Why go *back*?"

"Gloating. He's clearly gloating," Adele said. "Returning to the scene of the crime."

John muttered, "And sharing it with his sick little acolytes."

Adele wrinkled her nose, shaking her head. "Let's get out of here. I'm feeling lightheaded. Do you have a babysitter on the way for the apartment?"

John flashed a quick thumbs-up. Adele stowed her phone and, holding her breath as she passed the no smoking sign, she hastened back down the steps with John following her.

They pushed back out through the glass door, covered in fluttering notes and announcements taped to the window, and Adele inhaled the fresh air. John joined her a second later, this time holding his own phone out. "I sent his number—they're tracking him now. We can cut him off when he arrives in France. Train station is only an hour away."

Adele nodded in appreciation at Renee's quick thinking. Still somewhat lightheaded—which had nothing to do with her slowly healing stab wound... at least, so she told herself—Adele followed John hastily back to the car.

This time, he flirted with the other side of the speed limit, hastily racing through the city, one hand gripping the wheel, the other clasping his phone to his ear as he listened to instructions from the agent back at HQ tracking Gastone's phone.

Adele felt her head spin as she settled in the front seat, blinking a couple of times as black dots danced across her vision. She glanced down at her shirt and winced. A faint stain of red was leaking through. Slowly, so John wouldn't notice, she pulled the hem of her shirt, checking her bandage.

It wasn't bad. Just some minor bleeding. She'd replace the bandage tonight—it was fine. She could still help. John needed her, anyway.

Besides, after seeing their suspect's stream of the first victim's crime scene, listening to some of his obscene comments, she was more confident now that they needed to speak with Mr. Gastone.

Another thing had also occurred to her. The man was back on a train. If they didn't hurry, he very well might decide to claim his third victim.

"John, I'm fine," Adele lied, draping one hand past her side to hide the bleeding. "Go fast. Faster!"

"We can't outpace the train, Sharp," John said. "Gotta wait for it to

39

show up anyway. Gonna be hours."

"We'll meet it at a closer stop, then," Adele retorted. "Please—we can't wait. Go!" Another dance of dark spots, and she closed her eyes, turning to rest her head against the cool window.

She just needed a bit of shut-eye. Some time to clear her head.

But there just wasn't time…

John jerked the wheel sharply, the tires squealing as he pulled around a semi, merging onto a ramp. A horn blared, John shouted but then added quickly, "Sorry about that."

Adele just flashed a thumbs-up even as her stomach churned.

Perhaps she'd overestimated how quickly she was able to return to work. Not that it mattered now. No going back. Foucault was counting on her. This psycho's next victim was counting on her.

"Faster," she mumbled… And then her vision faded into darkness.

CHAPTER NINE

Adele jolted upright to the sound of more squealing from the tires. She blinked a couple of times and glanced over. Renee was still focused on moving through traffic. Now, though, they'd left the city behind them. The phone with their tech agent was on speaker now, and a voice was urgently calling instructions.

"That one, Renee! Yes, just ahead. Two minutes. No—one... The train will arrive in one minute. Are you almost—"

"There!" John shouted.

He pulled over a curb, and Adele gritted her teeth as she jolted. She glanced down at her bandage. No more blood. The stain from earlier had dried. Barely visible. Her head was still pounding, but she could think clearer now. The nausea had faded, along with the black spots. She'd just drifted off for a few minutes. That was all.

Her eyes darted to the dash clock. She'd drifted off for more than an hour.

But again, denial reared its ugly head and Adele just sat upright now, trying to focus. John was throwing the car in park. Ahead, she spotted a train station. French, though they must be in one of the northeastern border towns by the look of things. She didn't know the location based on the GPS indicator.

Renee glanced over at her sharply. "You alright?"

"Yeah, fine," she said testily. "Just drifted off. Didn't sleep well last night."

John hesitated, staring at her. She didn't so much as flinch, putting on her best poker face.

Renee just muttered darkly and shook his head. A few hundred feet ahead, Adele spotted a yellow and blue passenger train hastening toward their small, border town stop. Only a handful of commuters were waiting at this station, which was little more than two glass walls and an open ceiling with a kiosk.

John shot Adele a final look. Instead of pleading her case or explaining her impromptu nap, Adele shoved out of the car, stepping onto the curb and moving hastily toward the platform.

John followed behind. His phone was still in his hand, the speaker chirping.

"He's coming in now—do you see the train?"

"I see it!" John called back. "Which compartment?"

"It's not that accurate," the techie returned. "But we have locals stopping the train for now. It won't move until we give the go ahead."

John gave a nod at this. "Good shit. Alright, I'm hanging up. Call back if he moves."

John stowed his phone and, distracted by the notion of apprehending their suspect, seemed to briefly put his concern for Adele on the back burner as the two of them moved through metal turnstiles, which an attendant activated at the sight of their badges.

They both came to a halt on the platform just as the yellow and blue train squealed into the berth. There was a hiss as pressure released from the sealed doors' hydraulics, and a couple of passengers disembarked. An old lady in a shawl boarded the second compartment. But otherwise, there was little motion.

Adele's gaze darted between the two emerging passengers. One was a young man, but he didn't have the little pornstache she'd seen on the live stream. The second man was older with darker skin than Mr. Gastone.

She allowed them to pass, glancing at John and pointing further up the train where two officers had climbed the metal rungs to speak with the conductor. For the moment, the train would stay still.

But even from outside, glimpsing through the windows, Adele could tell it would be no easy feat to locate their suspect amidst the hundreds of passengers. Even now, a few of them were glancing out the windows, frowning. The doors were still open. They weren't moving.

Adele didn't want to wait for this air of disgruntlement to spread. She beckoned at John, gesturing toward the second compartment while she approached the fourth. There were five in total. All with two levels of passengers.

It would be like finding a needle in a haystack. But at the very least, they knew the needle *was* here. Renee moved off toward the compartment she'd indicated, pausing long enough to call to the cops, "Anyone gets off—stop them!" He raised his ID.

One of the cops hopped down from the metal rung, taking the instruction in stride and giving a quick nod.

And then Adele lost sight as she stepped onto the train. Her gaze briefly caught the dark gap between the open doors and the station platform. As she stepped over it, her shadow coming with her, she couldn't help but feel a faint chill along her spine. Something about the dark gap between the floors made her uncomfortable. Safety on either side, save the small sliver of danger or dismemberment in between.

There was a metaphor in there somewhere, but Adele didn't linger to discover it.

As she emerged in the compartment, she began glancing around, her eyes darting from face to face, scanning the passengers in their seats. She cataloged faces, postures, expressions. More than one disgruntled commuter. More than one irritated traveler. She could hear whispered questions now.

Why are we stopped?

Police? What police? Are you sure?

We should get moving soon. Maybe something is wrong with the doors.

She didn't stop to answer anyone, but instead made her way along the cramped hall, gaze moving back and forth like some sort of spotlight. He wasn't in the fourth compartment. She took the small curling stairs up to the second level, scanning this space as well.

A few napping passengers. One man picking his nose... No Mr. Gastone.

She frowned, hurrying back to the first level and moving on to the fifth compartment. John would hopefully check the second and first. They could meet at three.

But as she hurried along, glancing side to side, receiving more than one irritated glare or stuttered question, Adele maintained her focus long enough to realize their suspect wasn't in the fifth compartment either. Neither level.

She let out a hiss of frustration. Expressions of irritation were swiftly moving to boredom. Heads were lowering onto arms, searching for quick naps. Phones emerged where games were played. Pages of books fluttered, earbuds buzzed with the sound of music or too-loud podcasts.

But there was simply no sign of their suspect.

Adele could feel her anxiety rising. She fished out her own phone, moving back toward the fourth compartment, sidestepping a particularly wide commuter holding onto an overhead plastic strap.

"Got him?" John's voice spoke first.

"No—guessing that means you don't."

John growled. "Not in first or second."

"Not in fourth or fifth," she replied.

"Third?"

"Meet you there... actually, wait—hang on. Let me check something." Adele felt a spike of excitement as the idea hit her. Some people, when bored, reverted to entertainment like books or movies or even naps.

But others... especially the sort that livestreamed and took inappropriate photos for an online audience...

She cycled back in her phone to the link the station manager had provided. She clicked it, waiting for the web page to load. And once again, she found herself staring at a live video with chat spamming an adjacent box. But this time, there was no commentary. Just heavy breathing. The emojis flashed past. A few hearts.

Adele realized that Mr. Gastone was taking a video of a very pretty young woman sitting across the aisle from him. She spotted red seats and, on the other side of the glass, a police officer moving along the platform.

She shot a look out her own window. No police officer. She hurried forward, ducking her head out the open doors. She spotted the officer right outside the third compartment, strolling back and forth, his hands behind his back.

She referenced the video feed again. The officer was strolling with hands behind his back.

"Third compartment!" she barked into her phone. "Second level— he's on the second level, John!"

She hastened forward, still staring at her screen as if glued to the moving images. Ahead of her, as she hastened through the second compartment, she thought she heard the sound of shouting. A split second later, her speakers squawked on her phone as the video-feed amplified the voices.

"What do you think you're doing?" someone called from the third compartment. A second later, the same voice, equally shrill, buzzed from her phone.

Adele disconnected the stream, hurtling a poorly stowed piece of luggage and hotfooting into the middle compartment. She arrived just in time to see Agent Renee standing on the first level, but reaching up through the rail of the second level where he'd snagged a man by the ankle.

Mr. Gastone squawked and sputtered and protested as John dragged him by the foot through the gap in the rail. Gastone's phone tumbled from his hand.

"Help!" he screamed. "Attack! Fire! Let go of me, you bastard! You're all witnesses! All of you—witnesses!"

He tried to kick at John's head but missed and only managed to dislodge himself further from his seat. Agent Renee bodily lifted the man and carried him, one-handed, out of the compartment.

"It isn't nice to spy on young women," Renee was saying in a patient tone. He didn't even seem to notice the smaller man's slaps and pinches and punches. Most of the blows glanced off John's shoulder.

Adele sighed, stopping long enough to pick up Gastone's phone. She turned off the device, in case it was still recording, and then followed back through the doors, hastening after John and his squawking captive.

CHAPTER TEN

The small police station in northeastern France had fewer amenities than Adele was accustomed to. For one, the cops had only provided two chairs. John had insisted she take the seat, and Adele had been grateful for the chance to let her muscles rest, though she refused to display the extent of her exhaustion to Renee.

Now, John leaned like a gargoyle over the metal table, his long arms pressed to the surface on fists. Adele sat upright in her chair. She'd taken a moment before entering the room to wash at the stain on her shirt. Thankfully, her jacket hid it for the most part and Renee hadn't spotted it yet. She wasn't eager to have that conversation.

Now, both of them directed their disapproval toward a common enemy.

Mr. Gastone shifted uncomfortably, muttering darkly in the face of their unwavering attention. "Where's my phone?" he demanded.

Adele just watched him, maintaining her silence and allowing the intimidating presence of John Renee to do its work. The large man's shadow spread across the table, enveloping their suspect like some eerie embrace.

"I said where's my phone!" he yelled, his cuffs rattling where they scraped against the table.

"Mr. Gastone," Adele said primly, "we'd like to ask the questions."

"I'm going to sue you," he said.

What she heard was, *I have authority issues*. Everything from his shaking upper lip, the sweat beading on his forehead, and the equal parts angry but nervous glances he kept casting at them suggested this wasn't going to be an easy confession.

So Adele decided to start slow. "Sir," she said quietly, "I'd like to know what you were doing in Hamburg."

He snorted, leaning back. "Filming a crime scene for a new series I'm starting."

"A new what?"

"Series," he said, enunciating each syllable. "Now where's my damn phone?"

"What's on your phone, sir?" Adele asked. "Something you don't want us to find?"

"No! My life's work, lady…" He studied her for a moment, his sweaty upper lip curling. "You wouldn't understand."

"Understand why you take candid pictures of women without their permission?" Adele asked. "Why you visited a crime scene right after being fired from a *second* crime scene?"

He snorted. "That thing with the finger in the locker? They wouldn't let me film. Gestapo."

Adele sighed. John leaned in, glaring. "So you admit you tried to return to the second crime scene?"

"Return? What… like after getting fired? It's a train station, big guy. People have to use trains." He gave an exasperated shake of his head and shot a look at Adele as if they were sharing silent contempt. She kept her expression cold.

She spoke up now. "How did you know about the finger in the locker? I don't believe we've released that to the press…"

He looked at her as if she were stupid. "I still have friends that work there," he said. "Just because Barras is an asswipe doesn't mean everyone is."

"We were told you were fired for harassing a commuter. Your manager said you made threats when you left."

Somehow, Mr. Gastone managed to communicate contempt in nearly every motion and scowl. Now, he was rolling his eyes and letting out a sigh like a recalcitrant child. "I threatened to come back and push him onto the tracks. But it was a joke—I was live-streaming. The fans though it was funny. So sue me."

"He might," she said.

"Or we might just lock you up," John added. He straightened up, adjusting the top button on his collared shirt. "You have a history of stalking women. We saw your apartment."

At the mention of his place, the man went rigid.

Adele shifted uncomfortably, finding the pain in her side somewhat of a distraction. She forced herself to focus, studying Gastone. The mention of his place was clearly a sore spot. She kept her tone professional, even, and pressed on. "You've been taking pictures of women," she said, "and pasting them to your walls. How come?"

The man swallowed, his tongue darting between his lips and adjusting his pencil-thin moustache. "I don't know what you're talking about," he muttered.

"Same with the murders?" John asked. "You were at the crime scenes by accident. You know details of the case by chance. A lot of quick explanations for your behavior, sir. None of them particularly convincing."

Now, Gastone was breathing heavily. He shook his head adamantly, head a blur. "No, no—hang on. I didn't hurt anyone. You're starting to sound like you think I might have…" He trailed off and then visibly swallowed. "I wouldn't ever *kill* someone! What? Okay, right—look maybe I took a couple of naughty pictures."

"More than a couple," Adele commented.

"Fine! Fine—I have a bad habit. I admit it. I'm a slave to my desires—is that what you want to hear?"

"Is that why you attacked those women?" John insisted.

"No!" his voice screeched. "I didn't attack *anyone*. I swear it!"

Adele shook her head. "I'm afraid we don't find you particularly credible, sir. What were you doing at the second crime scene?"

"I told you!" he exclaimed. "I was there to show the fans. It was a field trip. Some fun. I told them all about the murder at my old work place and they wanted to see the first location. It was just some harmless fun."

"You find mutilating women fun?" John said.

"No—man, look, you keep twisting my words. I'm just saying I was *at* the place. That's it. At. There. Watching. Doing *nothing*. Just watching."

"You like to watch," John said. "I know men like you." He glared down, eyes hooded.

Adele sighed, massaging the bridge of her nose. "Where were you on Tuesday night, sir?" she said. "Were you in Hamburg the first time?"

"First time? First time I was in Germany in like ten years was today. Before you two manhandled me."

"Just answer the question."

"I did! And—wait… *Tuesday*? Ha!" His eyes suddenly brightened. He tried to slap the table but only ended up jolting his cuffed wrists. He winced, and some of his look of triumph faded. But not by much. "Tuesday night—of course! Wasn't me, and I had a room full of people who can prove it."

Adele and John went quiet, watching him. The tone he was using suggested she wasn't going to like what he said next. But she soldiered on regardless. "Where were you, sir? And who can vouch for you?"

"SA meeting," he mumbled.

"What was that?"

Louder he said, "A sex addicts meeting. Shit. Want me to scream it from the rafters? Jesus, lady—I'm telling you, I was getting some help for… er… well, something of a personal issue."

"Being a pervert," John provided, nodding sagely.

"What—no! Just—well, a bit of a... Anyway, not important. But I was in Paris, in a friend's basement, with seven other men on Tuesday. I couldn't have been in Hamburg." He leaned back, wearing a smug expression. Then, after a bit, like an actor remembering a forgotten line, he hastily added, "Ha!"

Adele let out a faint sigh. "What was the timeframe for that?" she asked.

"Eight p.m. to ten," he replied quickly.

She shot a look at John, who was glaring again. This man's online charm was somewhat lost on the two of them. But one problem was glaring: they had an *exact* timeframe for the phone call the first witness had received after discovering the severed ear of their first victim. The timeframe landed smack dab in the middle of Mr. Gastone's supposed meeting. Of course, phone calls could be made long distance, too...

Knowing she was grasping at straws, Adele said, "Were you at this meeting the entire time? Would people vouch for you?"

He glared back across the table, his expression smug once more. "Give me my damn phone back, and I'll give you the numbers for seven witnesses that will all say I was there the whole time. So..." He glanced at John, then Adele. "Can I go now?"

"No," they both said simultaneously.

Adele wasn't sure what the most recent statute was for inappropriate candid pictures, but she was willing to hold the man for a bit to at least check it out.

"We need those numbers," John said stiffly. "All of them. And if you're lying, I'm definitely mentioning it to the judge."

Mr. Gastone snorted, beginning to roll his eyes but then catching himself. He just sunk lower in his metal chair, cuffed arms crossed as best he could, leaning back and staring at the two of them with hooded eyes.

Adele pushed slowly from her chair, her stomach twisting now. She had a bad feeling about Mr. Gastone's alibi. He seemed too confident it would check out. Besides, they hadn't found any weapons on him or in his bag at the train. He was a creep, but not a killer.

They'd have to verify the alibi, of course.

But she was starting to get an uncomfortable sensation that it was going to check out.

She straightened fully, and without another word, turned, pushing back out into the hall in order to fetch Mr. Gastone's beloved phone.

CHAPTER ELEVEN

He took two sprinting steps, his feet striking stones and sending them skittering down the cliff-face ahead of him. His arms tensed, his eyes widened, and he felt a familiar surge of excitement.

Then, at full speed, he jumped off the cliff. The sharp rocks and dry, dusty ground below sped to meet him, to crack his bones and skull, to rip his skin and suck his blood. The jutting stones protruded like teeth from the terrain.

His heart was in his throat. His skin tingling. And then he ripped the cord on his chute. A sudden flutter, a wallop of wind, and then a quick jerking motion from the black straps looped over either shoulder. Suddenly, his parachute caught the wind, tugging him with it.

Then came the sudden lull.

This was always his favorite part... The jolt of fear followed by a sudden, sweet release, and then silence... And the silence lingered, swelling around him, rushed away on occasion by tufts of wind, but returning just as quickly to envelop his gliding form. His skin prickled, his cheeks stung from the cold of the air. He tugged at one of the triangular metal hand-grips, redirecting himself over the chasm, along the slopes.

His lips stretched into a grin like a dog he'd once seen peering out an open window on the highway. The thrill, the exhilaration sparked through him... but it lessened as his mind wandered, already acclimating to this new momentum.

And that was the problem. Nothing created a thrill quite like the hunt...

He'd stabbed that bitch. Buried his knife deep in her ribs...

But she'd survived. She'd even put up a fight. He had to hand it to Captain Renee—John sure knew how to pick them.

The survivor tugged on his leads a second time, veering closer to the cliff, closer to danger... but even this failed to rouse his excitement. He hadn't been idle since the failed attack... No—that wasn't his style. He'd already set up a meet with an old contact. He wouldn't be using a knife this time. At least... not *only* a knife. He would go to the address with a weapon he had more familiarity with.

The thought of a second shot made him smile. This time, he knew he'd be able to make Captain Renee suffer.

After all, that was the point of all of this.

Pain.

Renee was a tough one... so more than one screw would have to be tightened. But once the survivor was done, he had every hope that big, bad John Renee would be weeping like a schoolgirl. And if not?

At the very least the people he loved would weep on his behalf.

The survivor twisted in his harness, angling toward the landing spot he'd mapped out earlier. A grassy incline at the base of the cliff, leading to a valley.

He always came with a plan.

The wind whipped around him, pressing his jacket and shirt tight against his trim form. The breeze whispered and screeched in his ears. The trees below waved in greeting, or perhaps warning, like traffic control directing planes.

And the grassy runway itself beckoned as he dipped lower, lower, falling from the sky like some bird of prey.

CHAPTER TWELVE

John Renee sat in the break room of the Parisian precinct, frowning as Adele delivered the bad news.

She lowered herself into one of the cheap thinly cushioned seats, holding a Styrofoam cup of steam in one hand. "Alibi checks out," she said dully, her tone matching his own emotions.

"Shit," he said.

She nodded. Took a sip, lowered her cup, and exhaled.

He detected the faint scent of black, no sugars, no cream. He tried not to stare at Adele, but it was just so damn hard to keep an eye on her. In another life, she would have made a fine poker player.

She never seemed to let her emotions play across her features.

Now, though, as John studied, he spotted her jacket shift. Briefly, he thought he spotted a stain along her shirt, near her ribs. He stared, but Adele caught his gaze—though she pretended she hadn't—and shifted, buttoning her jacket.

He wondered if he ought to say something. Perhaps put his foot down, or threaten to call Foucault and have Adele put on leave until she'd fully recovered.

But this would only infuriate her. John was concerned about Adele. Very concerned. This wasn't normally his MO; he'd never been the one to show too much emotion. Or hell, even experience too much. No, feelings were best left bottled up and sipped in solitude just like his moonshine.

He crossed his legs beneath the small, round, plastic break room table. A thin sticker tried to pretend the table was wood, but he saw through the deception.

Adele opened her laptop next to her steaming cup, still determinedly ignoring her partner's searching gaze.

John returned his attention to his own computer screen.

"You get a head start?"

"Yup," he replied.

"So where are we at?"

He looked over the glowing blue surface of his computer. "Nada. Nothing. Our victims don't have much in common besides their gender."

Adele sighed, nodding as she clicked on her own device, navigating the files Foucault had sent them before. She paused, the blue light reflecting off her features in an unchanging color, suggesting she was staring at the same image for nearly a minute as he watched.

After a bit, John cleared his throat, and she looked up.

"Huh?" Adele said.

"What's caught your eye?"

"I…" She sighed. "I'm not sure. But it's the finger."

John had hurried past the image of the severed finger, but now, reluctantly, he scrolled back. "What about it?"

"Why's the ring missing?"

"I… oh, you mean that tan mark?"

"Yeah. I spotted it before. He took the ring."

"So?"

"So she had other items on her. Well… her body did. There was money in her purse. Why didn't he take that?"

"I mean…" John sighed, massaging his face. Adele had always been the one to focus on the details. "I don't know. Why do you think?"

She gave a faint shake of her head, still troubled. "You don't think…" She paused, but then pressed on, her words and exhalations causing the plume of coffee steam to waver. "You don't think this is all just some elaborate burglary, do you? Hiding a needle in a haystack. I once heard of a man cut to pieces with a machete for a fifty-euro watch."

"All of this for a ring?"

"Maybe."

"What about the first victim? She still had her ring."

"I… true. But maybe," Adele pressed, "our killer is after a specific type of ring. Expensive rings? Heirlooms? Antiques?"

"We don't know what type of ring the second victim had."

"I think we should check anyway. He took the ring. At the very least, it suggests a willingness to steal. Killers often escalate from smaller crimes."

John shrugged. He didn't disagree. "So what's the call?"

Adele bit her lip, considering their options, but then said, hurriedly, "We should investigate recently released burglars or thieves with a violent history. It should be easy enough. Due to their political status, crossing the border from Germany into Paris would have pinged on *someone's* radar. Especially by train."

John nodded, impressed. "Nice thinking. Alright, here, I'm already logged in. Let me see… How far are we going back?"

Adele pushed to her feet, still moving slowly, but circled the table to join John. She leaned over his shoulder, placing one hand as if to steady herself against his arm. "Don't worry about sentencing dates, only release dates. Anyone—at any point—who was put back into society in the last year."

"Year? That's a long time."

"But they need to have traveled from Germany to Paris," she said quickly. "In the last week."

John's fingers tapped away on the white keyboard. He'd never much enjoyed parsing through the information provided by the Transportation Authority, but over the years he'd learned a trick or two even on the more mind-numbing side of the job. Desks and John Renee were reluctant partners at best. He'd been known to overturn one or two in his day.

"Larcenists," he murmured, clicking a box, "violent history," he said, selecting a row of white-boxed search parameters, "recent release," he continued the narration, setting the date, "and recent travels..." He double-checked then hit *enter.*

As usual, the database processed quickly enough until it arrived at inputs from Transportation. John tapped his fingers against the keyboard, holding back an exasperated sigh. Adele's hand tightened on his shoulder suddenly, digging into the muscle, as the screen flickered and two results appeared.

John frowned, control-clicking each file and opening two tabs displaying the profiles of two ex-cons. Adele tapped on one of the data boxes. "Not him," she said. "They never let him on the train. Didn't board—see."

John grunted, graying out that result.

One left.

Now, both John and Adele were staring at the face of a middle-aged man with long, dark hair tinged in gray. One of his eyes pointed in a different direction than the other, and his lips were pressed tightly together as if he found the whole business of taking his mugshot quite tedious.

"Looks like..." John trailed off, quickly reading the information. Then he repeated, louder, "Looks like our guy was arrested ten years ago for robbing a jewelry store."

Adele tensed again. "Armed robbery too. He attacked a woman during the robbery."

John nodded once. "And there's his itinerary. Crossed from Germany into Paris Tuesday night."

Adele swallowed, letting out a faint sigh. "Night of the murder," she said. "We need financial records, credit cards... anything."

John looked at her, twisting in his chair. "We looking for his hotel?"

Adele shrugged. "He came into another country. With a name like Michael Schmidt, he's not Parisian."

"Staying with friends?"

She shook her head, pushing off his shoulder as if using it like a launching pad. "Worth checking either way. Financials, reason for travel... all of it. I'll call BKA and see if they have anything further."

John flashed a thumbs-up as Adele stalked back around the table, returning to her own computer while pulling her phone from her pocket.

John studied the lazy-eye in the photograph, frowning at the middle-aged man. Was he a killer? His arrest record was long—not just burglary or robbery, but a couple of small-time muggings in his youth. One sexual assault. John shook his head. This Mr. Schmidt really was a piece of work.

And currently, he was roaming Paris unaccompanied. Sometimes, it could take time for a prison to notify neighboring countries about a traveling criminal. Mr. Schmidt had slipped through the cracks, boarding a train from Hamburg to Paris.

And now two women were dead.

John scowled, lowering his head and lifting his own phone to make a couple of calls. The first step to stopping Mr. Schmidt was *finding* him.

CHAPTER THIRTEEN

Adele exhaled slowly, adjusting her body armor and reaching out with one hand toward the motel room door. She shot a look at John, who was at the ready, weapon in hand. He gave a brief nod, then jerked his head toward the door.

Adele hesitated, glancing back over the second floor rail toward the two police officers waiting as backup on the lower level. Another officer was standing in the parking lot, flashing a light through the front window of a rental vehicle they'd managed to track from the train station. Mr. Schmidt had booked the room in his brother's name, but had used his own credit card.

The last crime Schmidt had committed involved a weapon. Hence the body armor and the backup. She returned her attention to the flimsy door, inhaling slowly. And then she knocked, her knuckles reverberating against the cheap, wooden frame.

"DGSI!" she called. "Open up!"

Nearly instantly, they received a response. But not the one they'd been expecting.

A scream erupted from the room beyond—a female voice by the sound of it. Adele stiffened in response, rapidly thinking through their options. Agent Renee, true to form whenever a damsel was in distress, chose that moment to throw his full frame against the balsa wood door.

There was a loud crunch. Half the frame splintered in the cheap setting. John's leg went through the door. He cursed, yanking it back and kicking now. The door remained shut, but the center of the flimsy surface broke inward, not quite casting splinters, but more like flaking large chunks of glue and wood pulp.

"DGSI!" Adele called again, just in case.

The female voice was still screaming, clearly distraught. The cops below them were hastening up the stairs now, their boots clanging against metal steps. John was already shouldering through the shattered door, hunching his large figure to fit. More chunks of fragile material tumbled about him like enormous flakes of dandruff as he entered the second-floor motel room. Adele followed close behind.

"Oh God!" the woman's voice was shouting.

A man had perked up from where he'd been kneeling on the bed, completely naked. He looked back at Adele and John and cursed. "What the hell!" he screamed in German, his face turning red with anger and embarrassment.

A second later, though, he seemed to process they were police. His face did a one-eighty, back-tracking, if such a thing were possible. He cursed now, reaching desperately for a pair of pants over the banister, but missing. So instead, he flung himself off the bed. The mattress made a croaking sound of springs. The woman beneath the covers was sitting up now, too. Her face framed by long, dark curls, her green eyes bulging as she watched the two DGSI agents rush toward the bed, weapons raised.

But Mr. Schmidt didn't stick around for introductions. He flung himself, still naked, through the glass window by the bed.

Like the door, the window also shattered. This time, though, the pieces offered a bit more resistance, evident by the sudden yelp as Mr. Schmidt tumbled out the other side in a shower of shattered crystal.

A second later, Adele heard the sound of faint *tinkling* as the shards hit the pavement below. Amidst the sound, a far less gentle noise occurred: *Thump.* "SHIT!" Another *thump,* this one softer, suggesting perhaps Mr. Schmidt had run into something. Another German curse.

John had already raced to the window. Adele stopped by the bed, raising her ID. "DGSI!" she repeated. "Ma'am are you okay?"

The woman just stared. "I—I… fine!"

"Was he hurting you?"

She hesitated… "I mean… yes." She winced, speaking rapidly in French and shooting uncomfortable glances toward John and the two officers who had just arrived in the doorway. "But he had permission to," she whispered. "He pays well."

Adele nodded. Her eyes skimmed the woman's fingers. A small, golden band looped her ring finger. Adele felt a chill, but shook her head, refocusing and following John hastily to the window.

Renee had already cleared the jutting pieces with the back of his weapon and had flung a leg through. Now, he followed that leg, wincing and ducking, and using his fingers to push up on the wooden portion of the frame to avoid jabbing himself.

"Stop!" John shouted toward the asphalt behind the motel. "I said stop! Adele!" he yelled hurriedly. "What's German for—ah, shit. Never mind!"

He dropped from the window with a shout. Another *thud.* This time followed by rapid footfalls, suggesting John had maintained his feet.

Adele pushed out the window now as well, peering into the

darkening skies above the motel. Two silhouettes were sprinting breakneck toward a small, green park behind the motel. A park bench served as a springboard for the first silhouette as the man launched over a bed of roses, hurtling past a row of trees onto what looked like a bike trail.

Adele cursed. Mr. Schmidt was fast—especially given his age… and naked tumble out the window.

She spun on her heel, looking back toward the woman on the bed. "You sure you're okay?"

The woman just nodded quickly, pulling her covers up under her chin. Adele raced back to the front door, stepping through the broken remains and calling instructions to the two officers standing awkwardly there. "Please watch her!" Adele said. "Take a statement if she's up for it. Call paramedics!"

One of the officers snickered. "Don't think she's gonna need paramedics. Maybe an aspirin."

"Just do it!" Adele snapped.

And then she left them in her wake, hitting the curling metal staircase and taking the clanging steps three at a time. She hurtled down the stairs and rushed to the parked car they'd taken from the precinct. John had left the keys in the ignition in case they'd needed quick access.

Adele slipped into the front seat, put the car in gear, and peeled out of the motel parking lot, leaving rubber on the road. She then sped around the motel, through an alley lined with dumpsters and, tires screeching, sped toward the small park falling further under the sway of evening.

She sped straight over the park bench, wincing as it splintered and the car jolted. Ahead, she spotted Renee sprinting after the naked man through a pair of swings. The chains rattled as the two plastic seats went spinning. A couple of teenagers, whose domain was the park late at night, stared over pilfered brown bottles in stunned silence as the naked man and his giant pursuer rushed back onto the bike path.

Adele aimed to cut off Mr. Schmidt's escape route. Tires spinning, she kept to the path, rushing toward an intersection that led back to the main street. John had noticed her and was trying to chase their target in her direction.

As she threw the vehicle in park and emerged to try and cut the man off from the other direction, she heard the sound of John's screamed instructions. "Hands up! Stop running! Don't face me!"

Adele's own weapon emerged and she stationed herself in the

middle of the path, waiting for Mr. Schmidt to appear around the curving path where John was chasing him.

And then he appeared, like a bull facing a matador. For the briefest moment, he seemed to hesitate. His eyes widened. He swallowed, staring at Adele. And then, he seemed to reach a sudden decision. "I'm not going back!" he screamed. "I won't! I refuse!"

Adele kept her weapon raised, her hands steady. "Sir!" she yelled. "Stop where you are. Stop right now!"

But he didn't heed her. The nude German sprinted straight toward her, arms pumping. He didn't have a weapon. Didn't seem interested in attacking her. He just wanted to get past...

Adele remembered the last time she'd interacted with an unarmed suspect. Briefly, her thoughts darted back to the scene. A man in the water, bubbles rising on either side of his face. The sound of gurgling. Her own stomach in her toes. Her fear curdling her blood flow.

She remembered the way she'd shot the killer. Remembered the way she'd watched him die.

Now, as Mr. Schmidt came straight at her, she wasn't quite sure *who* she was looking at. Adele blinked, her side throbbing. She briefly lowered her weapon an inch. He was unarmed.

But he was charging her.

But he was unarmed.

But he was a dangerous criminal.

But he was unarmed.

"Adele!" John shouted. "Get down!"

The big man had his own weapon raised as he came in rapid pursuit of Mr. Schmidt. He would have a clear shot if she moved out of the line of fire.

But in his haste to catch up with the killer, and, Adele noted, an uncharacteristic hesitation on his trigger finger, Agent Renee made a mistake.

She saw it happen before she thought to shout a warning.

And again, it was clear he was trying to protect her.

But in this endeavor, he drew *too near* their suspect.

And Mr. Schmidt seemed to realize it.

Instantly, the naked man dropped to the ground, curling in a ball. This would have been fine if John hadn't been sprinting behind him breakneck on the jogger's trail. Prickling branches of uniformly planted trees swayed and shifted above them.

John cursed, unable to stop in time. His foot caught the suspect's flank. And then John's feet were introduced to his head as he went flying. In his fervor to keep Adele safe, Agent Renee had made a tactical mistake.

Adele hadn't seen such a thing before. Especially not from John.

Now, though, the big man hit the dust with a loud shout and painful grunt. Mr. Schmidt wasn't idle though. He lunged for Renee.

No. Not John, Adele realized.

For Renee's weapon, which had fallen in the collision.

Adele shouted, but was unable to get a clear shot. John tried to shove to his feet despite his collapse. He was blinking something fierce, wincing as he tried to move. Dust and dirt lathered the back of his shirt. Adele was still standing by the hood of their car, eyes wide as she fixated on the scene on the bike path.

And then Mr. Schmidt stood up, gripping a gun tightly in both hands, aiming toward Adele, then John. His eyes were wide, one pointing off to the side. His lips were pressed in that same thin line from his mugshot. He let out a cough, spitting dust and swallowing fiercely.

"I said," he rasped, "I *won't* go back."

John, who couldn't understand German that well, glared at the man, slowly trying to rise.

"No!" Mr. Schmidt screamed. "Stay down! I swear I'll—stay down!"

Adele's own weapon trembled. She didn't have a clear shot. John was too big—blocking the field of vision. She said, slowly, "Renee, he wants you to stop moving."

The suspect yelled, pointing his gun at Adele now. "Hey!" he screamed in German. "Stop it! Stop talking!"

She went quiet. John's eyes glared murderously toward the man pointing a gun at his girlfriend. Indifferent to his own safety, Renee tried to rise again. But the man with the gun surged forward, kicking out and catching Renee in the chest, sending him reeling back to the dirt.

For now, the only thing injured was John's pride.

But judging by the way that weapon was swinging back and forth, coupled with the complete lack of trigger-discipline, Adele wasn't confident things weren't about to go sideways rather quickly.

"I won't go back to prison!" he was still saying, murmuring it now, his eyes carrying a haunted quality. He gave a fearsome shake of his head. "I refuse. I won't!"

"Sir," Adele said softly, in German, her own gun still half-raised. Her eyes were unblinking, fixed on the man. "We just want to talk with you. We're not sure what we came upon back there."

He looked at her, stunned at her German. "You—are you BKA?"

"No," she said slowly. "DGSI. We're French inves—"

"I know what it is," he snapped, waving his gun. Adele determinedly tried to keep her attention on the man's face. She couldn't help but notice that prison hadn't really done any favors to his physique. She supposed stereotypes about prison workouts were on a participation basis only.

She kept her tone cool, calm, trying to soothe the man. She wanted to glance over her shoulder, hoping desperately one of the officers had the good sense to follow. Then again, she had taken a car and instructed them to watch the woman in the bedroom.

She let out a faint huff. The trees on the side of the path obscured any visual of the park or the swing sets. No sign of the teenagers either. She hoped they knew what was good for them, and had already beat a hasty retreat.

Now, though, the man with the gun was shaking his head. "Shit," he muttered. "Shit!" he said louder. "I'm not going back," he added, his voice fierce, his eyes steely.

"I get it," she said. "We can talk about it."

"No!" he snapped. "No talking." He pointed his weapon straight at John. "I will kill you both and myself before I go back. Are we clear? Now I want that car. Throw your gun to the side or I'll kill this moron."

CHAPTER FOURTEEN

John's teeth pressed tightly together. "What's he saying?" Renee murmured.

Adele didn't reply; she didn't want Schmidt to direct any more attention toward her partner. Instead, she slowly lowered her weapon, holstering it with cautious motions. Renee winced as she did. Now the only one aiming a gun was their suspect.

Adele felt a flicker of anger. John had been trying to protect her. But he'd been *over*protective. If he'd just kept his distance, just let her handle it…

She cut off the trail of thought. No… no use thinking like that. She was angry. But not at John. The situation was the issue. And if she didn't think quickly, the man was threatening to paint the ground with Renee's gray matter.

Adele's hands tensed at her side as she surveyed their suspect. From an outside perspective, it might all have seemed comical. A nude fellow gripping a weapon while two federal agents tried to deescalate.

At least… one of the federal agents tried to deescalate.

The other one kept trying to push to his feet and tackle the assailant and each time was rewarded with a shout or a renewed threat with a firearm.

After another attempt from John to inch closer, Mr. Schmidt just yelled, "Tell the French dog to stop! Or I'll put him down!"

Adele let out a fluttering sigh. "John… let me handle it."

Renee shot her an angry look. His eyes were narrowed, his breath coming in quick puffs. She'd seen him get like this before in life or death situations. John had an uncanny ability to shut down most of the reasoning portion of his brain in order to let the ooga-booga caveman loose.

And currently, the rock-chucking, fire-finding side of her boyfriend was eyeing the gunman for the best angle of attack.

"John," she said, more insistently. "Please, just let me…"

Something about the tone in her voice must have given Renee pause, because although he remained tense—half-kneeling as he was, he didn't move toward their suspect.

As for Adele, she wished she felt as confident as she sounded.

Backup was still far away. The assailant had demanded her car and threatened to shoot John if he wasn't given his way.

As far as tactical positions of strength, Adele felt as if she found herself on lower ground, in a muddy field, with no plan to speak of.

So she winged it.

It wasn't often she was given the opportunity to interrogate a suspect in the field. With good reason. But for now, she needed to distract him. To think. The best way she knew to put someone on their guard was to accuse them of something.

So she came out with it, full force.

"Why did you murder those two women?" she said, keeping her tone firm but calm. "Why did you mutilate them?"

The man blinked. It wasn't a surprised expression, nor was it an offended one. It was as if he'd been expecting this.

Adele felt a trickle of fear along her spine. A suspect with a gun was one thing. De-escalation remained on the table. A serial killer with a gun? Cornered and alone... chances of survival plummeted drastically.

"You killed in the Hamburg train station first. Why?"

The man didn't say anything, but instead was trying to circle around Renee's fallen form and move toward the parked sedan. Adele knew that if she let him into the car and allowed him to drive away, the chances of him leaving *two* perfectly useful hostages behind were minimal. Given the killers' interactions with women in the past, she wasn't certain she wanted to go anywhere with this man.

She stood her ground, watching him scoot along the road, keeping an eye on John and Adele at the same time as best he could.

She tried again, launching a new salvo. "What did she ever do to you? Paris was next? Why trains? Was there something about the trains that appealed to you? It's a public space, isn't it? How did you know where the cameras were to knock them out?"

The man finally glanced at her, reacting to the barrage of questions more than anything. "You're nosy," he said simply.

John contributed, "What's he saying?"

Adele ignored him and received a glare for her silence. But at least this way she maintained Mr. Schmidt's attention without reminding him of his threat to ventilate Renee.

"It's my job to be nosy," she said softly. "Why did you come to the room? Was the woman upstairs going to be your third victim?"

For the first time, the man's expression softened. "Scarlet," he said quietly.

"Excuse me?"

"Her name is Scarlet. We're friends. Or… well, I'm a client." He snorted. "I used to visit her before I went away."

"Visit?"

He rubbed at the side of his nose with the gun now. He'd managed to skirt past Renee and now stood in the center of the road. "She's a whore," he said in manner of explanation.

"Right…" Adele swallowed. "So she was going to be your next victim?"

He frowned at her now. "Get away from the car." He aimed the weapon at her. He stood about ten feet away from her and John, in the middle of the road where he'd managed to maneuver to, standing beneath the rising moon which twinkled through the prickling fir trees and illuminated the shivering blades of grass swept by low zephyrs.

With his back to Renee, John was inching forward again. But every so often, the suspect would shoot a look in the direction of Renee, forcing the big man to freeze. It was like a very deadly version of the child's game Red Light, Green Light.

Adele, for her part, was motionless. The longer she stalled, the better. She wasn't sure how to play this. She couldn't let him get in the car. She especially couldn't get in with him. She needed to offer him something he wanted.

Something else besides a getaway vehicle. Clothes might be a good start… But as she considered it, she settled on another option.

Slowly, so he could see her hand, she reached for the radio clipped to the edge of her bulletproof vest. "I can get Scarlet to come speak if you like… She might want to see you before you leave."

The man snorted. "How stupid do you think I am? Now get away from the car. Where are the keys?"

Adele pretended like she hadn't heard, furrowing her brow as if in deep concentration as she clicked the radio. "Hello," she said slowly.

Mr. Schmidt tensed, his finger on the trigger. "Stop that!" he snapped in a fierce whisper.

Adele held up a finger as if to ask for a moment. She said, faintly, "Would you mind letting the woman out on the porch, as long as she's well. I think we need to speak with her."

"I said stop that!" Schmidt yelled at her.

Adele quickly raised her hand, lifting it from the receiver. She could only hope the cops in the hotel room had been listening. In the distance she heard the sound of rapidly nearing sirens, suggesting at least they'd followed the instructions to call for paramedics. Hopefully they'd had the good sense to ask for more backup as well.

Mr. Schmidt's cheeks were red with rage now. He kept moving toward Adele, slowly, cautiously, eyes darting to the weapon in her holster, his hand gripping Renee's gun with white knuckles.

John, for his part, followed an inch at a time, keeping as quiet as possible.

Adele remained motionless, standing by the vehicle, desperately calculating the likelihood of their suspect leaving without using that gun of his.

According to his arrest record, he'd once bludgeoned a woman half to death with the butt of a gun for refusing to empty a cash register. He also had a sexual assault charge. Though the man was exposed, and the situation was an unusual one, Adele didn't need reminding that Mr. Schmidt was a threat. By the looks of things, he'd mutilated and murdered two women, and had been planning to do it again. Maybe not with the prostitute in the hotel, but certainly with someone else.

She *really* couldn't get in that sedan with him. But what if he threatened to shoot John?

She shot a look over her shoulder toward the balcony, desperately hoping the cops had been listening. She needed something to help calm the situation.

"I'll give you one last chance!" he snarled. "Keys or I start shooting."

Adele winced. "Keys?" she said in German. "I'm sorry, my German is slipping. What is that?"

He bit his lip, his finger tight on the weapon. For a moment, she thought she'd stretched her luck too far. But then, he cursed, spitting off to the side in disgust and snapped, "Keys! Keys! They go in the ignition. Vroom! You speak German fine. Give them here."

"Oh," she said, pretending to smack her forehead. "Keys. Of course. They're in the car."

He glanced sharply toward the vehicle, scowling.

"The lights are off," he snapped.

"I turned them off," she replied. "Didn't want you to see me approaching."

"Yeah, well, how'd that work for you," he muttered. He was now sliding around the hood of the car, moving hastily toward the front seat.

Agent Renee was moving too, though. Adele's eyes widened. She refused to look directly at her partner and give up the game, but he was moving in a crouch, picking up speed, rapidly approaching Mr. Schmidt from behind.

She wanted to shout at John to stop. Wanted to raise her own gun.

65

Suddenly, a voice cried, "Michael! Are you okay?"

A woman's voice, coming from the motel balcony facing the small park. A dark-haired woman with green eyes stood on the small balcony, next to the shattered window, peering out into the dark, squinting as if she couldn't quite make out their shapes. She wore a bedsheet wrapped around her twice, and the two cops behind her watched sheepishly. At this distance, with the light pollution from the room, they hadn't yet determined the situation either, it seemed.

But the woman's voice seemed to do it.

Mr. Schmidt had been in the middle of turning to check on John, but at the shout from Scarlet, he brightened, looked up at the balcony.

"I'm fi—" he began to say.

And then two hundred and fifty pounds of ill intent and bad manners struck him from behind. The gun went flying. Adele felt like a sprinter at the start of a race. She'd been standing motionless, but at the sudden strike, she burst forward, sliding over the hood of the car and rushing to Renee's aid.

Mr. Schmidt was trying to punch John, but Renee had him face down in the dirt, hands behind his back.

"Stop it!" John snapped. "Stop resisting! And dammit, someone needs to find him some pants. Adele?"

She was breathing heavily as she pulled her cuffs, handing them to her partner. "I'm not giving him mine," she said sarcastically.

"Har, har. Tell one of those useless boots in the room to grab them. I don't want him sitting in the car like this."

Their suspect's voice was muffled by a mouthful of dirt, and Adele wasn't listening anymore either. The woman on the balcony shouted, "Michael! What happened! I heard something."

Adele spotted Renee's weapon just beneath the car. She bent to pick it up, but John beat her to it, grabbing it with a quick motion and sheepishly holstering it.

"Shit," he muttered.

"About right," she said.

"He confess? I couldn't understand."

Adele gave a faint shake of her head. "He threatened to kill you."

John glared at the man as he cuffed him. He hoisted the fellow roughly to his feet, and Adele hurriedly moved toward the balcony as John kept their suspect in a firm grip, pressing his bare chest against the cold metal of the car so he couldn't move.

Adele reached the base of the balcony, carefully avoiding the glass. The two cops stared down at her. Adele said, "Pants?"

One of the cops blinked. "The suspect's pants!" she clarified. "Please?"

An officer held up a finger, hurried back into the room, and returned a second later with a pair of cargo shorts which he tossed over the railing. Adele grabbed them, nodding in gratitude.

Sometimes, even to her, the job was strange.

Scarlet, though, was crying, tears streaming freely as she now had a good view of where her lover was being held against a vehicle.

"He didn't do anything!" she protested. "Why are you hurting him?"

Adele looked up at the woman. "Ma'am, I'm afraid you don't know who you're dealing with. That man was going to kill you."

She scoffed. "Michael? Ha! I've known him for more than a decade. He'd never hurt me."

Adele shook her head. "Be that as it may, he killed two women. Did you know that?" Adele's eyes narrowed. "He just murdered someone last night at a train station."

At this, though, the woman on the balcony snorted, muttering a series of less than flattering terms often attributed to police by people on the other side of the law.

Adele frowned. "Excuse me?"

She wondered how it must have looked, standing amidst shattered glass, holding cargo shorts and looking up to speak with a prostitute on a balcony. Perhaps not the *most* classy reenactment of Rapunzel.

But the woman was scowling. "He didn't *kill* anyone last night!" she snapped. "He was with me!"

Adele shook her head. "Ma'am, it was at the train station. After he arrived in Paris."

But she scoffed again, shaking her head even more adamantly and causing her luscious girls to bounce. Her green eyes flashed angrily. "Not possible!" she snapped. "I picked him up."

Adele swallowed. "What?"

"I," she tried again, slower, "picked," she said, "him," she narrowed her eyes, "up."

"What time?"

"The moment the train arrived. About ten at night. He spent the evening with me. Like I said, I've known him a very long time. He pays well. Besides, he hasn't stolen anything since he was released."

"He only got out this month," Adele pointed out.

"Still," Scarlet retorted. "He's a good man."

Adele sighed, considering the arrest record. She didn't like growing cynical with the job. A large part of her suspected that most people, as they aged, regretted the worse things they did in their youth. She certainly did. But she'd also seen the things Mr. Schmidt had *done* to earn himself a stint in prison. People had been harmed, sometimes severely.

Still, she couldn't let her own assumptions bias her.

She let out a shaking breath, then said, "You're telling me you picked him up *directly* from the train station?"

An adamant nod.

"There's no chance he slipped off before—"

"None. Why would he? He was coming to see me. We'd been planning it for months. Ever since he heard he was paroled."

Adele let out a long sigh. She wasn't sure if she could believe the source. It wasn't like Ms. Scarlet didn't have a bias. But would she cover for a murderer?

Adele's eyes darted to the ring on the woman's finger... Smaller than the band from the tan line of the Parisian victim. But what if she was in on it, somehow?

Adele shot a look back toward the vehicle. John was waiting impatiently, gesturing for those pants while leaning away from his suspect in a desperate attempt to avoid touching the naked man.

Adele sighed, returning her attention to Scarlet. "What about later?" she said. "Is it possible he snuck out of your—"

Another scoff. "Not with what *we* were doing. He didn't sneak *out* of anything. Let me tell you."

Adele winced, turning again and rubbing at the back of her head. She felt much like Mr. Schmidt had. Caught between two threats. On one side, she knew their suspect had just threatened to kill John. But he'd clearly exclaimed his reason, hadn't he?

He didn't want to go back to prison. But even as she'd interrogated him, while he hadn't been surprised, that didn't mean he was guilty. He certainly hadn't admitted to anything. Perhaps, like any reasonable person, he'd seen the news, connected the dots, and known the feds would come.

Maybe that was why he'd run.

Then again, on the other hand, what if Scarlet was just lying? What if—

Her phone suddenly began to ring. Adele hesitated, feeling a prickle along her fingers as her hand hovered over the device. She let out a faint breath, pausing long enough for the phone to ring a second time. Now, in the distance, she could hear Renee's phone also ringing over the sound of the approaching sirens.

Adele reached into her pocket, her knuckles grazing the cotton as she finagled the phone and quickly answered. She kept the cargo shorts at arm's length.

"Hello?"

"Agent Sharp?" Foucault's voice said.

She winced. If the boss was calling, it meant something serious had happened.

"Sir?"

"Where are you?"

"In the field—arresting a suspect."

"Well," Foucault's voice replied, somewhat testily, "I hate to be the bearer of bad news, Agent Sharp. But you have the wrong man."

"How do you know that, sir?"

"Because," Foucault snapped, "the killer is currently on a line with a commuter in Belgium. He's been talking to the man for nearly twenty minutes. He found a body part. The body hasn't been found yet."

Adele felt as if she were melting with each subsequent word.

"A… body part…" She trailed off, trying to make sense. She shot another look toward John and their suspect, then glanced up at Scarlet.

The woman looked smug. Though she couldn't hear Foucault, she clearly could read Adele's expression, probably from a lifetime of vetting clients.

Adele frowned. "Sir. You're sure?"

"Agent Sharp!"

"Yes, yes, of course, sir. We'll be right—wait, Belgium, you said?"

"He's still on the line. He seems to be enjoying himself. We're stalling. You need to rush."

"Sir, I'm not sure how quickly—"

"Where are you?"

Adele glanced toward the motel, searching for a number.

Foucault let out a huff. "Have local PD take care of your suspect. You two are going to Belgium. I'll book a damn private plane if I have to. Hurry. The police there have agreed to stall, but I'm not sure if they'll be able to keep him interested."

Adele felt her heart sink, her stomach soon to follow. "They found a body part? Which one, sir?"

Foucault let out a whooshing sound. His voice shook if only for a split second, but he swallowed, recovered, and said, "A foot. The killer is trying to lead the commuter to the body, but he hasn't yet, thanks to quick thinking by the Belgians. They're trying to stall to track the number."

"Is it working?" Adele took a sideways step, her foot scraping through glass.

"For the moment, stalling is. But he keeps changing numbers and calling. We aren't able to track. Now text me your address. I'll personally book you a flight. I'm serious—drop everything and go!"

Adele looked up at the police in the window. She pointed toward John and their suspect. "He's yours," she said. "And make sure the woman sees a paramedic."

Then Adele spun on her heel, hastening back toward Renee, cargo pants flying in the night like a flag.

CHAPTER FIFTEEN

The watcher's smile was out in full display as he leaned back in his La-Z-Boy, viewing everything unfold across his laptop screen. He'd even set up a custom wooden desk upon which he'd set his computer. Next to him, a small glass filled with cherry juice shifted, ice clinking as he swirled the straw.

He took a sip of the delectable nectar, all sweet and tart and frigid. He let out a smacking sound, followed by a long *ah!* And then he returned his attention to the business at hand. The small train locker flashed with the white light from his camera. The foot of his latest ex sat beneath the lens, just in frame. The small metal container pulsed with the glow of the strobing camera light and echoed with the sound of his breathing.

He knew they were stalling.

Knew the police had arrived hours ago. But it was just too much damn fun not to play along. He spotted the same passenger who'd first discovered the foot in the locker. The man had wide eyes, pale skin, and a twitching mouth.

He emerged in frame once more, staring into the lens. He blinked owlishly, his lips tight, his expression one of nausea. All of this was part of the fun.

The watcher enjoyed his audience, still breathing and waiting. The ground beneath his desk was littered with broken phones. After five, ten minutes he shattered the burners and started another one.

This was his eighth call in the last few hours. Each time he rang, the commuter appeared again. This, if anything, was a giveaway about the police presence nearby. There was no reason for the old, sallow-faced man to stick around. Not unless someone was *making* him.

And the Belgium police force was the perfect candidate.

The watcher smirked as the man's head bobbed into view, disappeared, then returned. His lips were pressed so tightly, they'd nearly vanished.

He waited a second, simply savoring the moment. And then he reached out to his computer, scrolled through the various voice options, and clicked one. The software was cheap enough—easy to find online. He ran it through a VPN, hiding his IP. The microphone attachment he used on each new phone was also untraceable, but perfectly hid his voice.

Now, a growling, demonic, booming voice echoed from the phone in the locker ten miles away from where the watcher had booked a motel.

"You need to help her," the evil voice exclaimed.

The man squeaked, staring wide-eyed into the locker over the foot.

"Help her!" the watcher shouted. "She has to be found. Return her foot to her, if you must…"

He held back a choked giggle, trying to stay serious. But he often smiled and he often saw the humor in most things. Especially all of this. And fear, to him, was the funniest thing of them all.

People practically bled the stuff, breathing it out into the world with each staggered gasp. Their eyes held terror. Their bodies trembled with it. Sometimes they even stank of it.

He didn't have the same enjoyment over the phone and video as he did when up close and personal with his ex, but this was the next best thing. Plus… he glanced at the small, blinking red light in the corner of his screen… this was the gift that would keep on giving. He could rewatch the man's terror as much as he wanted.

Already, he'd clipped more than an hour. An hour of absolute delight. He eagerly watched the camera on the second burner phone that he'd placed next to the severed foot, waiting for the man to speak.

Would they be rehearsed words like the last few times? Or would the old fool finally summon some nerve and improvise.

"I…" the man stuttered in broken English. "I don't know what you want. Who are you?"

The watcher frowned now, leaning back in his chair. A rehearsed line then. Pity. He was hoping for some fun.

He glanced at the small, hockey-puck-shaped timer by his computer. Eight minutes was almost up anyway. Undoubtedly, the police would be searching the station for the body. He had made sure to hide it well, though. Would any of them check the luggage racks? Time would tell. He kept refreshing the local news on his computer as well.

He let out a faint sneer. "Useless," he snapped.

And then he hung up. He shattered the phone, cracking it in half then flinging it at the floor. He stomped a couple of times for good measure then reached for the hammer leaning against the bottom drawer of the oak desk. Swinging this with some difficulty, he smashed the phone and kicked it under the knee-gap for the desk, sending it skittering to join the other rejected devices.

Then, primly, he set down the hammer again, reached out for a new phone sitting in the small pink bucket by his computer, inserted the battery pack, and booted it up.

Then he called the number once more. The image on his screen continued its feed. He'd managed to bypass the app from shutting down when it received a call, so the video-sharing connection maintained. Again, this was run through a powerful series of VPNs.

There was no way they could find him.

He waited as the phone rang.

Then the old man picked up…

Except it wasn't the old man. A new person had come center stage, staring into the metal locker, frowning over the foot.

A blonde woman—pretty with somewhat exotic features. A sharp nose, high cheekbones, and a small chin. Behind the woman was a man built like a brick wall.

The wall was muttering something to the woman. Was that in French?

He smirked. This time, as he connected the small mic attachment, he reached out and clicked a new voice on his software. A buzzing, humming voice intended to sound like a cartoon.

The watcher felt this fit the moment. A funny situation with a funny voice. He smirked as he said, also in French, "Nice of you two to come out of the woodwork. Have you been lurking behind the scenes *all* this time?"

The woman didn't reply right away. Her eyes were moving, constantly darting about. She stood straight, shoulders back, face motionless save the eyes. These cataloged everything, noted every detail. He wasn't sure he liked the woman's expression.

He tried again, louder. "You must be police!"

The woman again didn't say anything. He frowned now. Was she trying to get a rise out of him? She was pretty… though a bit older than his ex had been. The big man was scowling into the camera lens, murmuring again in the woman's ear.

Watching the way the two of them stood by one another, the large man standing protectively near the smaller woman, the watcher felt a flash of envy.

He remembered that posture. Remembered that sense of safety. It was all gone now.

"If you don't want to talk, then I'll leave. Find her yourself," he snapped, some of his good humor vanishing. He never could quite explain why his temper did this. One moment, calm, collected, the next lashing out.

It was one of the reasons things hadn't worked out with his ex.

Strangling her to death had been another small reason. His thoughts cast back, and the memory played across his subconscious in high-definition. He savored it. The sort of memory meant to be enjoyed, but never shared.

"You know where the body that belongs to this foot is?" the woman said at last, also speaking immaculate French.

What were the French doing in Belgium? DGSI? Most likely. He'd snared a big fish this time. He was determined to have his fun.

"You know I do," he snapped. "You know who I am."

"I'm afraid I don't," she said. "Who are you? What should I call you?"

"I don't mean that," he said. "You *know* who I am. What I am. That foot is my gift to you. Of course I know where the body is." He giggled, allowing the sound to buzz through the voice emulator.

The woman shook her head. "My name is Adele. There, I've properly introduced myself. Don't you want to?"

He snorted, muttering, "I'm getting bored. Very bored. Is that the best you have? Trading names?"

The woman didn't say anything to this. Instead, she glanced at the man next to her. The big fellow leaned in, speaking as well now. "Where did you hide her?"

He was enjoying the game... but on the other hand, it had been hours. Besides, he had a train to catch. "I'm not sure I want to tell you that," he said. "What's in it for me?"

"I don't know," the woman replied. "Why don't you tell us, and we'll see if we can help."

He chuckled. "You'd like to help me, hmm? Women always say that."

"Is that why you kill them?" the lady named Adele replied just as quickly. "Because they're liars?" She didn't blink. Didn't hesitate. If anything, she was trying to get a rise out of him.

But he wasn't stupid. He hadn't gotten this far by being dumb. Besides, he was starting to get irritated. The big man was standing too close to the pretty lady. The pretty lady was talking as if they were friends. But they weren't friends.

That had been the problem that set it all off. He wasn't trying to be anyone's *friend*. He gritted his teeth now, fingers twisting against the plastic of his new burner phone. He glanced at the small timer on the desk he'd set for five minutes this time.

Soon, the clock would run out. He hadn't yet had his fun, though. He changed the voice software, switching to a crying baby voice. "I bet you want to know how to find me," he said in a singsong tone. "Bet you want to catch me."

The woman said, "Maybe we can discuss this in person. Would you like that?"

He snorted.

She tried something else. "Why don't you show us where you hid her? That way we can all leave happy."

"But I'm already happy!" he declared. "Can't you tell?"

The woman paused. Then, ice in her tone, she said, "People who are truly happy don't generally have to insist it. Are you here? In Belgium?"

"I think we've talked enough," he said, ignoring the question and glancing at his timer again. "It's been fun. We should do it again sometime," he added, injecting some level of mockery to his tone. "And again... and again... and again."

He giggled now, slapping a hand against his knee out of mirth. And then, deciding he didn't like these two, he hung up. He cracked the phone. Stomped it. Smashed it with a hammer. And then pushed to his feet, moving toward the trashcan so he could dispose the smashed phones. He'd of course wipe down every piece. Everything.

He'd check out in the next twenty minutes. And then catch his next train.

There was nothing they could do to stop him.

CHAPTER SIXTEEN

Night had fallen completely, and with it, Adele's mood also darkened. Two murders in a single day. She turned her back to the locker in disgust, breathing heavily, refusing to look in the direction of that blinking white camera light. She pointed toward one of the Belgium police officers standing nearby. "Turn that thing off," she said. "Don't smudge fingerprints." She spoke in English with the correspondent who'd picked them up from the airport.

The man hastened over, intent on complying with the directive.

Elsewhere, further down the hallway of the above ground train station's employee structure, more police were moving in and out of the employee showers.

Someone had found blood. This, of course, was one of the reasons she hadn't insisted on keeping the psycho on the line.

Judging by the exclamations and shouts from the direction of the showers, they'd found the body.

She marched away from the lockers, shaking her head and running a hand through her hair. Three murders in three days. The killer had been taunting her. He'd been *enjoying* it. The voice scrambler, now that she heard it first hand as opposed to via police report and witness testimony, wasn't some military grade tech—it had been a joke. He'd changed voices for fun.

That was one thing she'd picked up on. The sheer sense of *enjoyment* emanating from the phone. He'd been watching them, getting off on it.

She moved past two Belgian officers, flashing her badge when they slowed, frowning after her. She reached the door to the employee showers, and then she spotted the suitcase beneath a changing room bench. A large suitcase. The zipper was slowly opened.

She spotted a face… The rest of the body. Another woman. Though Adele had guessed as much based on the foot and MO.

She stared as forensics took pictures of the suitcase and the corpse, moving to capture the gruesome spectacle from multiple angles.

Adele didn't linger back. She needed to know.

She marched up to the suitcase, ignoring the faint protest of one of the forensic girls. She leaned in, careful not to contaminate anything.

She just had to *see*.

She stared at the victim's hands…

And there she spotted it.

A wedding ring. Left on the hand. A vibrant, bright ring with a large diamond. An expensive ring.

The killer hadn't touched it. He'd had time to kill her. To strangle her to death and cut her foot. But he hadn't taken the ring.

Adele let out a frustrated sigh, turning on her heel and moving away again. What was she missing? What was the killer up to? Was he just playing games? Having fun through his murder spree with no rhyme or reason?

The tan line around the finger from the second victim still bothered her.

But maybe that was beside the point. If the killer was just teasing them, it didn't much matter *what* his reasons were. Perhaps he had none.

He was certainly prepared. The line always went dead before they could track him. He'd taken out a camera in the Parisian station. He knew what he was doing.

She shook her head, glancing back to where Agent Renee was in conversation with their correspondent, using stilted English. She approached and John held up a finger, quickly excusing himself from the conversation and turning to face Adele.

"Find it?"

She nodded.

"Dead? No—never mind. Of course she's dead. I… shit. Our guys aren't having luck finding the phone either. He must have destroyed it."

Adele sighed, nodding. "He knows what he's doing. And he's enjoying it. I could hear it in his voice. It wasn't just feigned humor to mock us. Though there was that. But he actually was having genuine fun. Like this was all some game." Her hand bunched at her side and she jammed it in her jacket pocket if only to do something with it.

"So what next?"

"Forensics will go over the body," she said.

"Missing ring?" John said hopefully.

"No. Ring was on."

Renee's face fell, mirroring the emotion Adele had just experienced for herself.

"Shit," he said.

She nodded. "I don't get it… He's taking *some* things but not others."

"Wait... *things*?"

"Yeah," Adele said, pointing toward the locker. "Look at the ankle."

John wrinkled his nose, but complied with the request. He frowned for a moment, peering into the locker now that the phone had been removed and turned off. It took him a second but then he spotted what Adele had earlier.

"Tan line," he murmured.

"An anklet, I think," Adele said. "Some girls wear those."

"Some guys do too," John muttered. There was no doubt in his tone what he thought of this. "So he took an anklet... took a ring from the second victim... But what about the first one? The woman in Hamburg?"

Adele lingered for a moment, rubbing a hand through her hair, trying to think clearly. Then, suddenly, an idea struck her. "John... where is the first victim currently?"

"*Where*? At the coroner's in Germany. Why? Shit... you don't want to take *another* flight, do—"

"No—no, we can call," Adele said. "We might need to go through BKA to wake up the coroner. But we need to call. I think I have an idea. I think the coroner might have missed something."

"Like what?" John said, reacting to the clear urgency in her voice.

But Adele was already dialing a number. A BKA contact who'd fancied John. Agent Marshall was her name. Adele hastily dialed, moving away from the lockers, distancing from the hubbub by the showers.

John's footsteps tapped behind her, hastening to keep up. It was late, very late. But a little bit of sleep was a small price to pay. The killer was striking rapidly. A murder per day. They didn't have time for sleep. Didn't have time to hesitate. If Adele was wrong, it was just more time wasted. Time they had very little of.

But if she was right...

Her heart hammered as she waited for the phone to connect, praying that Agent Marshall would answer.

CHAPTER SEVENTEEN

Adele yawned, staring at her phone as she waited for her BKA contact to connect her with the German coroner. She'd returned to the car, sitting in the dark sedan in the parking lot at night. Renee sat driver's side, watching her phone with something between a frown and a look of anticipation. The night was steadily creeping to the a.m., but Adele didn't have time for rest. She watched the small, rotating loading symbol buffer as the call connected.

Agent Marshall had been unavailable, but her partner had been awake. Rousing the coroner had proven something of a difficult task, and now Adele owed more than one German operative a favor.

If not for her father's reputation in law enforcement, and her own experience working with BKA, she wasn't sure the call would've happened.

But she *needed* to know. An anklet taken from the last victim. A ring from the second.

The first, though, had been found with her jewelry still attached. An earring was even in the severed ear… But sometimes, one simply had to look under the appropriate rock.

And for the moment, she was kicking stones.

Finally, the video connected.

Adele blinked, reaching up to turn on the light in the vehicle to help illuminate the dark form she presented in the video.

A faint shiver crept up her spine at the thought of the last person who'd watched her on video, but she focused as the German coroner stifled a yawn, yellow curlers in her mop of brown hair.

"Yes? This is Dr. Febar." The woman on the other line yawned again, holding a hand up to her mouth and closing her eyes for a second.

Adele waited politely, then gave a little wave into her webcam. "This is Agent Adele Sharp with the DGSI. Here is my partner, John Renee."

The coroner didn't reply, just waiting.

Adele kept her own tone professional. "I apologize for the late call," she said.

"It *is* late," the coroner cut in.

"Yes, well, we're working a case with Interpol, and it involves the murder in Hamburg."

The coroner sniffed, waving a hand. "I know it. She came in a couple of days ago. The Van Gogh."

"The—oh, well, yes. The woman with the severed ear."

The coroner rubbed at her sleep-deprived eyes, a couple of her hair curlers shifting. "How can I help you, Agent?"

Adele could feel John watching her now as well. Swiftly, she replied, "I have gone over the photos you supplied, but I need to see the woman's ear if possible."

John stared. The coroner stared. Adele just waited patiently.

"The ear?" John said.

"The ear?" the coroner asked.

"The ear," Adele returned.

Again, the silence stretched, though this was in part due to the poor internet connection.

The coroner gave an exasperated sigh and a quick shake of her head. "I don't just have availability to…" She paused, trailing off and frowning. Her face froze again as the pixels spasmed, but then the video feed returned mid-sentence as she said, "…maybe for now… Alright, alright. One moment." She pushed to her feet, judging by the suddenly shifting angle of her camera lens. Then came the sound of tapping footsteps against cold tile.

A few more moments passed, and Adele spotted a long row of cooling compartments. There was a sliding sound, and then the coroner's face popped back into view.

"For preservation purposes, I can only give you a few minutes. What do you need to see?"

Adele was practically shaking now from anticipation. Her eyes fixed on the screen. She swallowed faintly, and then in a whisper of a voice, she said, "Does the ear have a second piercing?"

The coroner frowned. The camera shifted again, revealing the ear in a metal tray. John looked away as if ready to be sick. But the coroner was just murmuring, as she pointed toward the ear. "There's the piercing right here," she said. "It should have been in the photos I sent."

"Yes!" Adele replied quickly, her own fingers darting absentmindedly to her ears. She'd once gotten them pierced in high school but eventually let them close up again. Some of her friends had taken to the piercing process with gusto, though. This, in particular, was why she was here. She hesitated faintly, then said, louder, "Can you check the cartilage?"

"Hang on," John said. "The piercing she had—we have the earring, yes?"

The coroner held up a finger, moved, and then returned a few seconds later with a small, plastic evidence bag she set on the table. "Didn't get it to the detectives yet. Didn't think an earring was that urgent."

"No," Adele said, "it's fine. We're not looking for the earring she had. We're looking for the one he stole."

John was now watching Adele with a curious expression. The coroner held up a white-gloved finger and returned her attention once more to the item on the table. "Cartilage?" she said. "I mean, I'm sure I would ha—oh."

Adele's heart skipped at this last syllable. "What is it?" Adele insisted, leaning forward in the motionless vehicle. Her mouth came so close it even fogged the glass. She hastily wiped away the mist. "What's the matter?"

The coroner was frowning, shaking her head. "I don't know how I missed it. Well, no, I do actually. It's tucked *under* the ear line. Hidden from sight. But yes—there's a small piercing. No earring, though. Which is why I missed it, I'm sure," she added defensively, glaring into the camera.

Adele just flashed a reassuring smile. "Thank you!" she said. "Could you send us photos of the piercing, please? Both? Thanks!"

Then she hung up, turning sharply to John.

He looked impressed, studying her. "So... all three of them had jewelry that was stolen."

"Exactly!" Adele exclaimed.

John massaged his chin. "I... don't... why is he only taking certain jewelry?"

Adele pointed at her partner, her skin still buzzing, her eyes wide in the dark vehicle. "Not just that," she said. "He's cutting the body parts off where he takes the jewelry."

John winced. "Which comes first? The jewelry or the body part?"

"Exactly the question," Adele said. "If we discern that, we discern part of this psycho's motive." She gave a giddy little tap dance of her feet against the carpet beneath her, beaming through the windshield now, feeling a genuine shift in their prospects.

The killer had been mocking, taunting, one step ahead. But she felt like they were finally gaining on him.

As she considered this, though, her smile faded somewhat, and her frown returned along with a descending brow line.

Knowing *what* wasn't the same as *why*.

She held up a finger in front of her face, murmuring softly as she spoke. "A missing ring on one," she said. "A missing earring on another. And a missing anklet... The killer is only stealing *some* jewelry... but not others... What if there's something about the jewelry itself? What if it isn't arbitrary?" Adele said, turning to look at Renee. "Killers always have their reasons. He's gone to meticulous detail to plan out and execute his attacks. So *why* go after just those jewelry pieces? Why has he never brought it up? Never taunted us with it?"

John shrugged. "Embarrassed?"

"Or scared," Adele said. "Embarrassed or scared or..." She shook her head. "I don't know. But if he's hiding the jewelry that means it's the first place we should look."

"Only problem," Renee shot back. "We don't have any of it."

"No... But we have the next best thing," Adele murmured.

"What's that? The video of his hand in the lockers after he turns on the camera? He's always ducked out of sight, though—it's just a gloved hand. No jewelry, and no—"

"No," Adele cut in. "Tan lines. Marks. Distinct tan marks on the body parts, like charcoal etchings of leaves. Maybe not as detailed, but we have the ring and the anklet. It should help identify at least the *type* of jewelry."

"We know the type, though," John said quietly. "An anklet and a..." But even as he said it, he trailed off. "Oh... I... I actually might have an idea."

Adele perked, her blood bumping rapidly. She just waited quietly as John's brow furrowed. "Remember that old contact of mine we visited on our earlier cases? The one in that basement of the cafe..."

"The one we threatened?"

"Right... Well, he has a fence he works with who deals in stolen jewelry."

"A fence?"

John waved away her look of hesitation. "He's also an expert in the craft. He knows everything about every piece of glinting or glistening ornamentation that comes through the city. He once identified my watch by the sound of its *tick*."

Adele felt the same sense of excitement coursing through her once more. "You think he could identify the type of jewelry our killer is taking?"

John shrugged. "Worth a shot, at least. He works late, too. If anyone can identify a piece of jewelry off a tan mark, it's Buggo."

Adele wrinkled her nose. "His name is Buggo?"

John snorted. "No, that's just what we call him because of his eyes—you'll see."

Adele glanced at the clock on the dash. By the time they took a flight back to Paris to meet this contact of Renee's, it would be well past one in the morning.

"Exactly how late does this guy work?"

Renee was already procuring his phone with a knowing nod. "As late as needed if you know what to say. I'll make a call. You book the flight."

Adele gave her assent to this work distribution by flashing a thumbs-up and returning her attention to her own cellular device. She felt as if they had fresh wind in their sails. Now they just needed a little direction.

The killer was striking rapidly, one day after the next... which meant they had to be faster still. Sleep would have to wait.

CHAPTER EIGHTEEN

Adele couldn't stifle the yawn this time as she followed Agent Renee down the dingy Parisian sidewalk in one of the more cramped sections of the city. The usual farm of large, blocky, beige buildings and oversized streets was now replaced by geometrical patterns of city planning, which created long chutes of streets and cramped sidewalks tended to by the moist air from the river.

Ahead, a small path led beyond a bus stop missing half its steel partitions. John took the steps with sure-footed motions, and Adele followed cautiously behind him. A bridge spanned the river, arching above them. The water itself was dark and caught stray reflections from tall buildings and winking stars. Otherwise, the water just moved along in quiet, swirling patterns, unobtrusive as it went its merry way.

Adele yawned again, holding a hand to her lips and glancing at her phone, as she didn't wear a watch. The flight, the taxi, the trek… it was now nearly 3 a.m.

"Christ," Adele murmured, staring at her phone. "You sure this guy is still up?"

John walked with long, rolling steps ahead of her, carving the way toward his contact. He pointed with a long finger toward a small houseboat jouncing on the faint current, attached to metal posts beneath the bridge.

Adele stared at the wooden houseboat. It was hard to determine a color in the poor light, but the top half looked something like a double-sized garden shed with a slanted roof. The boat itself curved up on either side, creating a large, bulbous front portion, compared to a sleek, boxy back section. Adele had never spent much time with nautical terms like port, starboard, stern… She'd heard them, knew *of* them, but she wasn't sure she wanted to set foot on that treacherous-looking thing.

"Did you tell him to wait for us?" Adele said, walking brusquely along the river path in her efforts to reach the boat.

John hesitated, scratching his chin. "Ah… I mentioned I might have some business for him."

Adele shot her partner a look. "The jewelry thief?"

"A fence, technically."

"What sort of business would you have, Renee?"

"I didn't give *my* name. If I'd given my name he would've refused to meet... or set up an ambush."

Adele went very still, reaching out and snaring Renee's sleeve. She looked him dead in the eyes. "Ambush?" she said testily.

John waved away her concern with a flutter of his fingers. "Don't worry about it," he muttered. "It's fine... well... mostly." Renee swallowed, shooting a look back at the houseboat. "I mean, it's not like he knew it was *me* on the phone." Renee tried to flash what he seemed to think was a charming smile. It only managed to further frazzle her nerves.

Adele shook her head, muttering darkly. "Ambush..." she said beneath her breath. "Just great."

She approached far more slowly now. Hand on her holster as she cautiously drew nearer the illegally moored vessel.

John went more quiet the nearer they came. He often got like this when on the alert for danger. And while it always felt good to have John at her side in dangerous situations, Adele was having a hard time thinking straight. The pain in her side was pulsing with each step. Her exhausted form and mind were desperate for sleep.

If John's fence *did* ambush them, it might prove a welcome respite. Ending up in a hospital bed didn't sound *so* bad. It had the word "bed" in it, after all.

As they reached the boat, coming to a stop by the rail, a light suddenly flashed over a doorway in the main shed-like structure centering the vessel.

A single, naked bulb pulsed two times over the door.

Adele froze. John stared.

Adele recovered first, whispering, "Is that some sort of code? What's the response?"

John looked as if he'd been called on in class while passing notes to his crush. He stammered, stared, then muttered, "Dunno."

"John!"

He shrugged.

The light flashed again, more urgently this time. John gave a faint shake of his head, sighed heavily, then stepped onto the boat. Due to the massive man's size, the vessel swayed and rocked a bit. The light bulb over the doorway no longer flashed.

Adele stared past Renee, eyes fixed on the entryway to the main compartment.

No further sights or sounds.

Once she felt the coast was clear, Adele reached out, fingers against the spray-dappled metal rail. She hopped nimbly over, her feet hitting the wooden deck with a *thunk*. Thankfully, the boat didn't rock nearly as much at her arrival.

For a moment, the two of them stood on the deck, facing the doorway. Adele hesitated, then murmured, "Can you give him a call? Tell him we're here?"

John wrinkled his nose, his features cast in shadow. "I... I'm like fifty percent sure we're on the right boat."

She turned to look him full in the face. "We might *not* be on the right—"

Suddenly, the door slammed open, the wooden frame striking the wall with a loud *bang*. A figure emerged from inside, a weapon gripped tightly in his hand, aimed toward the two of them. "Definitely not the right boat, Johnny!" the man shouted as he stepped onto the deck. "What the hell do you think you're doing here?"

The man's voice was an octave higher than Adele had expected. He had long, stringy hair like a sweaty metal guitar player. He was bare-chested, boasting a skinny, rail-thin body. His eyes were larger than any she'd ever seen, bugging from their sockets. Every time he blinked, it was as if the orbs flashed out of view, then returned again like headlights on an oncoming car.

These large, bulging eyes moved from John to Adele and back. The gun, though, remained fixed on Renee.

"Um, hey, Buggo!" John said, giving a little wave. He didn't sound too perturbed by the gun waving in his face. "Nice to see you again, bud."

"Shut up!" the high-pitched voice retorted. "We're not *buds*. You sunk my last house!"

John gave a nervous chuckle. "I... ah... I forgot about that." He whispered to Adele, "This *is* the right place."

Adele's own hand hovered along her weapon. She waited, watching, tense. She didn't reply to Renee. Didn't want to give him the satisfaction. He'd been doing his best to protect her, to keep an eye on her. So she knew whatever he'd brought her into wasn't a threat as far as Renee's calculations went.

Then again, John didn't always define words like "danger" or "threat-level" the same as most. And now, the harmless fence who was supposed to help them solve their case looked ready to put a couple of holes through her partner.

As the boat rocked and swayed, and occasional flecks of chill liquid

86

splashed over the rail, Adele watched for any opportunity in case Buggo decided to lower his weapon.

John was still speaking, though, clearly attempting to defuse the situation. "Look, man," John said, "I'm not here to sink your house again. I actually have a job for you."

The stringy-haired man with the gun just glared at this suggestion. "I don't need your work!" he said with a shout. "I know better than to work with the mob now. Thanks to you."

Adele shot John a look. "The mob?" she mouthed.

Renee winced. "Ah, yeah, about that, Buggo—I'm not with LaGrange's outfit. That was a farce. A ruse. Pretend. I'm actually a DGSI agent." John said this last part with a dramatic pause and faint tilt of his eyebrows.

The fence just stared, licking his lips nervously. "What's Dijesay? New gang?"

"No. DGSI," John said, slower. "A federal agency. I'm a cop. This is my partner, Agent Sharp."

Adele flashed a thumbs-up if only to have something to do.

The man stared at both of them, mouth unhinged. "You're a *cop*?" he said.

John nodded. "I can show you my badge and everything."

"I don't buy it! No way! You're as crooked as they come. I saw you kill that man!"

"Buggo, I was working undercover. That *man* was a CI. He's doing quite alright and living happily on a beach somewhere. I'm not here to arrest you. I genuinely have work. Paid work."

At the mention of pay, the fence's mood slowly shifted. He let out a faint sigh, running a hand through his greasy hair. Then he lowered the gun. It took Adele a second to realize her mistake as Buggo pulled the trigger.

Instead of a blast, there was a soft splash as liquid sloshed across the deck.

A water pistol painted black.

Buggo chuckled at the looks on their faces. "A guy can never be too sure," he said. His eyes narrowed. "But I'm going to need to see that badge, or you two can get the hell off my boat. And I'm calling this in—you might be pretty to look at, Johnny, but I don't trust you an inch."

Adele sighed, waiting as Renee fished his badge from his pocket and held it up so Buggo could see. The man clicked something in his pocket and the lightbulb above his head turned on. The illumination cast a shadow toward Renee, but also shone on the identification in his large hand.

John's contact leaned in, studying the information. Adele yawled again, her hand relaxed on her holster now. At least it didn't look like they were going to get shot. But she was having trouble keeping her eyes open, though the same couldn't be said for the fence.

His orb-like eyes blinked a couple more times, like a camera lens, taking in the ID. He glanced at Adele, at her weapon, at her suit. Then he let out a faint, shuddering sigh.

"Shit," he said. "You're really a cop?"

John nodded.

"So Santo is still alive? For real?"

John nodded again.

Buggo looked happy about this news. He nodded once. "Good. I liked the guy. Shit—well, fine. Paid job, you said. What can I do for you, Johnny?"

Agent Renee just pointed a finger at Adele. It took her a second to realize this was her cue. Adele quickly pulled her phone from her pocket, cycled through to the high-definition coroner pictures, and said, "We need you to take a look at something for us. Images of jewelry."

The man chuckled, rubbing his hands against each other. "Shit, jewelry is something of my specialty, sweet thing. Has Johnny told you about me?"

Adele shook her head. "No, sweetie," she replied sarcastically. "He hasn't. Just so you know, the images aren't very nice."

She turned the phone toward the man. The moment she did, he let out a squawk like a crow and cursed. His face went pale. For a moment, he couldn't seem to look away, his gaze fixated on the images.

Adele cycled through the picture of the anklet and the finger. She didn't show the ear, as the markings were nearly nonexistent.

"That," he said, pointing after a moment, "isn't jewelry. Is this a threat?"

"Not a threat," Adele said wearily. "We don't have the jewelry. We were wondering…" She swallowed, realizing how silly it sounded now that she was saying it out loud. But they'd come this far, stayed up this late… it was still worth a shot. "Wondering if you might know *what* sort of jewelry these women were wearing."

"I don't see women," he muttered back. "I see a science experiment…" But he trailed off and sighed, shaking his head. "Fine, fine," he muttered. "One moment. Let me see." He reached into his pants pocket and pulled out a pair of spectacles. He perched these on his jutting nose, only further magnifying his oversized eyeballs. His thin bony bare chest went still as he held his breath, like a sniper before a shot.

Focused, he peered in, reaching out suddenly and grabbing her wrist to hold it in place. She tensed against his cold, clammy touch, but it looked as if he were simply trying to stabilize the image. Nose only a few inches away, he studied the pictures. He swiped from one to the next, muttering darkly and shaking his head. At last, he let out a sigh, looking up.

"I... just so we're clear," he said, "these are body parts. You can't judge my expertise based on—"

"Not here to judge you," John called from behind Adele. "Just looking for a bit of help."

"Yeah? And how you going to pay me, big guy?"

"We have a whole branch of our office for that," John returned. "I'll give you a number. Now focus—is there anything about those pictures that stands out? You saw the tan lines, right?"

"Yeah—dummy. That's not the problem. I saw the anklet mark and the wedding band. I also know that ivy pattern—you can tell by the leaf-shape protrusions. It's a unique one. But that doesn't mean—"

"Hang on," Adele interrupted. "Leaf protrusions? What's that?"

He hesitated, biting back an acerbic remark toward Renee and instead glancing at her once more. "That," he said delicately, "can show up in a couple of patterns..." He muttered beneath his breath quickly, saying things like, "Gauging for faceting volume, or if there's black opal... well, no—because that's clearly not a crescent clasp. Shit... What's that?" He leaned in again, eyes blinking behind his enormous spectacles.

He let out a sigh, twisting his head one way, then the next.

"What?" Adele asked, her voice tinged with excitement. "Do you know what it is?"

He looked up with a snort. "Hell no," he snapped. "It's a damn *tan line*, sweetie. What do you think I'm gonna find? But... well, I can't tell you the type of jewelry. And I can tell you that whatever it was, both items came from the same line. Or at least similar. How come you don't have the jewelry itself?"

He glanced between the two of them, his eyes magnified to such proportions behind those glasses that he looked something like a barn owl, staring at them.

"It was taken," Adele said curtly. "But back to the other part. What do you mean same line?"

"Oh." He waved airily. "I mean that the patterns match. See?" He pointed at the severed ankle. Swiped his finger along the screen and indicated the ring mark. "There's that little protrusion at the top. But then also at the bottom on the back. Leaves. Or vines. Or something similar. It's a pretty common pattern, except not with the crescent clasp." He pointed again. "I can't tell you much else. I don't know the material. Don't know if there were stone settings. Shit, I can't even tell you if this stuff is worth a buck. But there it is..." He trailed off and added a shrug for good measure.

Adele felt a flicker of excitement rising once more. "So," she said, pressing, "if they're both from the same line, what line is it?"

"Oh... I mean... I could come up with a list. But there's a lot of companies that make anklets and rings with vine patterns."

Her heart fell at this declaration. She tried to think through what she was being told. It didn't make much sense. The killer was targeting based on some stupid leafy pattern? Why so particular? She let out a huff of air. "Well," she said, "what about these?"

She cycled through the images to the jewelry items that had been left on the victims. All of them sitting in plastic Tupperware on metal trolleys.

Now, the fence's gaze brightened. He gave a cursory little lick of his lips and smirked. "Well," he murmured, "now we're talking." He tried to take her phone for a closer look but this time Adele slapped his hand. He winced but kept studying the images. "Those," he said, pointing to a couple of the second victim's earrings, "are butterflies with rubies in each wing. Not the most expensive, but nice. That one, however," he said, pointing to a wedding ring, "is at least ten thousand, easy." He snorted. "Man, is that why you've come? Wanna make a little change on the side, Johnny?"

Renee just rolled his eyes, his features illuminated in the glow from the light over the door. But Adele was shaking her head now. "Hang on, so some of the items he left behind were valuable?"

"Psh. I'd say. Very nice stuff. Why? I... I didn't sell any of this, did I?" he said, suddenly, panicked. "Shit—is this a sting?"

"No," Adele said, exhausted. "I..." She trailed off, desperately trying to piece it all together. Their killer was taking certain jewelry but leaving others. He had a penchant for this particular pattern, whatever it was... So financial gain was clearly out as a motive. But they'd already determined burglary was off the table.

She clicked her tongue, then had a sudden hunch. Jewelry lines generally distributed multiple types of ornamentation in their lines. But some excluded certain types. Anklets, for instance, were not a very common adornment.

She said, "So this vine pattern... are there any lines that include earrings *and* anklets *and* rings? Specifically wedding rings."

Now, the man was frowning at her. "Earrings? What earring?"

"It's not shown yet. We only just found a cartilage piercing. But focus—is there anything like that?"

"A line that also includes..." He Paused, then suddenly clicked his fingers. "I mean... well, I can think of two. But one of them is based in the United States."

"Forget about that one," Adele said quickly. "Not unless it would commonly sell here."

"French buying American wedding bands?" he snorted. "Please. No... not common at all."

"So what's this second brand?"

"Well, I only remember it because of the story."

Adele went quiet, feeling a slow chill at the way he spoke.

The man was glancing off now, frowning. He gave a faint shake of his head. "Huh. Funny thing. I was just talking about the company last week."

"What company, Buggo!" John called.

"It was called Sheen and Splendor," the man replied. "It was up and coming—making all sorts of names for itself. I tell you something, when I got a hand on a couple of those items, I sold them for a *real* pretty profit." He suddenly coughed. "All legally, of course."

"Of course," Adele said. "But what about Sheen and Splendor? Where is it located?"

"It *was* located here in Paris. But it's now defunct."

Adele's heart was playing yo-yo in her chest, bouncing up and down. She tried to bite back a scathing retort. She took a breath and said, slowly. "A defunct jewelry brand?"

"Yeah. They were doing well for themselves then out of nowhere they shut down a year or so ago." He shrugged. "I still had a couple bracelets in my very legal inventory. The scarcity bumped the prices. I'm not complaining."

Adele rested a hand on her hip, glancing over the edge of the rail. While the fence might not have been complaining, she very much wanted to. What good was a defunct jewelry brand?

Why would the killer target based on such strange parameters?

Was he?

Or was she missing something obvious?

She gave a faint shake of her head, letting out a huffing sigh. It was very hard to think clearly while holding back a yawn and wincing against throbbing ribs.

"I mean, the ivy marks was a hallmark of the brand," the fence muttered. "If that helps."

Adele paused, considered it, then nodded once, her head bobbing in some certainty. "It does help. I don't know how much. But you say this Sheen and Splendor brand was located in Paris?"

"Mhmm. I don't know the exact address. Shouldn't be hard to find online."

Adele fought back a yawn but glanced at Agent Renee, watching him expectantly. John just shrugged. "That all, Buggo?"

"That all?" he snorted back. "I just identified a jewelry line based on tan lines on severed body parts. You should be applauding me. Don't think it's free, neither. I expect that number. My fee has doubled besides."

"Of course it has," John muttered, pulling his phone out. But Adele was turning away, her mind something of a haze, her thoughts flitting like sparrows. She carefully stepped over the rail once more, grateful to have her feet back on the shore again.

She didn't even think to bid a farewell. Didn't turn to look back as John settled up with their contact. Didn't even wait for Renee as she began strolling beneath the bridge along the river walk, heading away from the two of them, putting the strange house boat in her own wake.

Her eyes were focused on what lay ahead. Exhaustion weighed heavy. Her footsteps felt slow. John called after her, jogging to catch up as he also left the boat.

As she took the sidewalk, moving back to the stairs, her mind was already a few steps ahead. If she was right, if the killer was targeting his victims based on their jewelry, then it wasn't out of some desire to crater the brand. Sheen and Splendor was already under the water.

No, this was a far more personal motive.

Whatever made the killer hunt would only propel him to further violence. Their only clue was the now-defunct jewelry brand. But in order to research, to think clearly, she needed at least a couple hours of sleep. Her place wasn't far from here.

It might be nice to have him sleep over anyway. That way he wouldn't keep bellyaching about her apartment's safety measures. At least not for now.

And after a couple hours of rest, then she'd find out everything she could about Sheen and Splendor and determine *why* its jewelry was prompting someone to kill. Not to mention the potential list of victims had turned into something of an avalanche. Anyone who owned a piece of jewelry from this particular line could be next in the killer's crosshairs.

CHAPTER NINETEEN

Adele wasn't sure if one was supposed to reheat bags of already popped snacks, but she also didn't have time to make a proper breakfast.

She blinked sleep from her eyes as she paced back and forth in her kitchen. John's snores echoed from the couch in the living room, reverberating over the sound of the whirring microwave. The faint scent of stale popcorn lingered in the air.

She and John had managed to snatch a few hours of sleep. He'd been more than happy to sleep on the couch to keep an eye on her. To his credit, he hadn't even asked to share the bed. The two of them had spent nights before, but this time the goal hadn't been pleasure.

And John's snoring would have prevented any amount of sleep.

Now, feeling somewhat rested, Adele clicked through the browser on her phone, frowning as she did. The first search term had seemed obvious enough.

Sheen and Splendor.

But the main result had led to a now-defunct web page of the once high-end jewelry brand. But the masthead of the site made it clear the site was now obsolete.

She reread the small band of text.

After three wonderful years of serving our clients, we are sorry to say S+S will be closing indefinitely.

That was it. No explanation. Nothing.

An up-and-coming jewelry brand had cratered for no apparent reason.

Adele tapped her foot against the ground as she paused by the microwave. Her nose wrinkled, and vaguely she thought she smelled burning. A faint wisp of smoke was wafting inside the appliance above the brown bag.

She reached out, clicking the door open and grabbing the reheated popcorn. John's snoring continued to rumble from the living room.

She grabbed a mouthful of stale corn and butter and then returned her attention to her phone, cycling back to the first page of search results.

A few more links led to other items on the obsolete website.

Customer service. Product pages. An About section which was now deleted…

She moved on to the second page of search results. A few blog posts in French were bemoaning the surprise end of their favorite brand. Some angry reviews mentioned how they hadn't been able to return products that hadn't met expectations.

But then, scanning the second page of results, Adele went still, frowning at a news article at the very bottom.

Adele tilted her head. The article wasn't dated. It looked more like a hastily transcribed archive file. But what *did* stand out was the content of the article.

A missing person. Someone who'd, according to the small amount of text, once worked as a clerk at S+S.

Adele frowned. She tried searching for more information on the article, but clearly it hadn't gained much internet traction. She found herself pages into results sorting through spam.

So instead, with a sigh, she grabbed another handful of popcorn and moved hastily over to where she'd left her laptop on the kitchen table.

She didn't have to rely on the same search results as most did.

She opened up the DGSI database with her two-factor credentials and then quickly narrowed recent case history by a missing persons tag.

She narrowed the missing persons by keywords, including things like "Sheen" and "Jewelry" and "unsolved."

There was a single result.

Her heart skipped. She slowly lowered her phone, setting it against the varnished table. John was no longer snoring. He looked up from the living room couch, glancing into the kitchen, blinking blearily.

Adele wiped her greasy fingers off on a napkin for the sake of her laptop, and then settled at the table and clicked the single result.

A name. *Bernice Wallen.*

And under the name, a driver's photo of a smiling, beaming face with braces. The woman looked to be in her mid-twenties, despite the general stereotype of braces being for the young. She had kind eyes, even in the still image. Her hair was neat, combed, her business suit professional. Adele glanced at the scant details of the report.

Bernice Wallen had been working for Sheen and Splendor for all three years of their meteoric rise. She went missing, though, sometime in her third year. Minimal information came out about the disappearance.

No one seemed to know anything.

The case was now cold.

Bernice had never been found.

But something else had caught Adele's attention. The date of the disappearance.

It was listed as only *one* day before the jewelry brand mysteriously closed down. She frowned, cycling back to the general search page online, double-checking what she'd found.

But indeed, Bernice Wallen had vanished from the face of the earth—and then just thirty-six hours later, the highly successful jewelry brand owner had shut down his business.

This was what, in the field, they called a suspicious coincidence.

"Morning!" John called, his voice deeper than usual in the a.m.

"Get dressed!" she shot back. "Please," she added. "Also, do you want popcorn?"

John blinked, yawning, holding up a finger and then saying, "I'm not sure how I feel about a hot chick telling me to put more clothes on."

"John, I'm serious," Adele said. "I think I found something."

He must have detected the excitement in her tone, because Renee immediately began pulling on his pants. She gave herself a brief window to watch her boyfriend get dressed. Spending the night hadn't been about fun...

But that didn't mean she couldn't enjoy the view.

When he caught her looking, he wiggled his eyebrows, and she smirked. But just as quickly, the expression died on her face as she looked back at her computer. She hastily moved toward the door now, grabbing her sidearm from where she kept it under the coat rack. Closer to the door now, but hidden. Just in case any more late-night visitors stopped by.

John was dressed, but his hair was a mess and he had bags under his eyes.

She shot him a look. "You look old, Renee."

"You look old," he said.

"Good one."

"Good one," he replied.

She snorted. He winced. "Sorry... brain isn't fired up yet. I can write a few comebacks down if you like. I'll read 'em off over the course of the day."

She patted him on the cheek. "You seem alert enough. I have a lead."

"A lead?"

"Like a *lead* lead," she said, still excited. Then, out of sheer delight, she leaned in, gave him a quick kiss, wrinkled her nose, and said,

"Actually... I'll start the car. You brush your teeth."

He frowned, breathed into a cupped hand, inhaled, then winced. "I think that might be smart to spare us both. See you downstairs..." As he hastened back toward the bathroom, he paused, shooting a look over his shoulder. "Make sure the cop is still in the lobby."

But Adele just waved a hand as she opened the door and stepped out. "I'm fine!" she said. "Don't worry about me. And hurry up! We have a jewelry store owner to visit!"

CHAPTER TWENTY

The adrenaline junkie sat on the hood of a car, pretending to listen to music and adjusting at the white earbuds with gloved fingers. Every so often, though, he glanced from beneath the upturned hood of his sweatshirt toward the small garden behind the chicken-wire fence.

A child was playing in the garden. She couldn't have been much older than ten years of age. Claudia... Her name was Claudia. He'd heard the girl's mother shouting from the window.

He watched the little thing hurry around the yard, moving from one toy to another. Just like her father, she never seemed to be able to sit still. At least not for long.

He watched with hooded eyes, slipping off the hood of the car now and continuing his jog around the trail. He'd already spotted the camera over the door. There'd been another camera on the back door. The windows had blinking green lights—a security system.

John Renee's ex sure knew how to lock down a fort.

If he didn't know better, he might have suspected they'd had trouble in the past. With a connection like Renee, this was hardly surprising.

He rolled his shoulders as he picked up the pace, jogging along. He moved just out of the angle of the door camera. As he passed the small fence of the equally small home, he flashed a grin toward the kid.

Claudia was watching him now, pausing where she'd been jumping on a trampoline. He gave a little wave, his fingers curling.

Her eyes widened and she hopped off the trampoline, racing into the house.

This only prompted him to pick up his pace, smirking as he moved. It didn't matter if some strange jogger had scared the girl. One way or another, he was going to get what he came for.

There was only one thing that currently motivated him.

John Renee's pain.

Captain Renee had never mentioned a family. Never talked about a daughter. He supposed this made sense, as the girl wouldn't have been much older than a few months at the time of their last deployment. The time of the betrayal.

His eyes narrowed, his teeth clenched. He rounded the jogging path, taking a route through the small wooded trail. He picked up his pace now, moving from a jog to a sprint, allowing his anger, his flash of memory and fury, to spike through him.

He didn't move as quickly as he once had. His arms didn't go as fast. His shoulder still throbbed and ached every time he took a step. Each price tag of pain, though, he would exact from Renee's own skin. The tab was running and the bill would soon come due.

CHAPTER TWENTY ONE

Adele tried to pick a piece of popcorn from her teeth as she simultaneously admired the large mansion behind the cluster of garden hedges.

"Big house," John said from her side.

She nodded once. "Very. A very rich man lives in that big house." She leaned forward, her fingers vying for the buzzer hidden by dangling ivy. She pressed it a second time and stepped back once more, returning to her stance on the sidewalk where she peered up at the enormous home.

"So let me see if I'm understanding this," John murmured, eyes darting through the bars of the gate as he tracked the small hedges lining the pavement. "This missing woman *worked* for Mr. Weeks?"

Adele nodded. "Worked in his main store for three years. Then vanished without a trace."

John snorted. "And Anton Weeks shut down his business?"

"Like the day after."

John just looked at her. "Basically he's admitted it already."

Adele shrugged. "I guess we're about to find out." She stepped forward to ring the buzzer a third time, just as a small speaker in the ivy crackled to life. A voice snapped. "What?"

"Hello, is this Mr. Weeks?"

"Who the hell am I speaking to?" the voice said. Some of the words came jumbled and slurred.

Renee held a thumb to his teeth, miming a drink. Adele kept her tone polite. "DGSI, sir," she said.

The moment she did, she heard the man on the speaker yelp as if he'd been scalded. Her brow flickered, but she didn't comment on the odd reaction.

"I... I'm busy," the voice said, clearly rattled now. She thought she detected the faint hint of panic.

"Be that as it may, sir," she said softly, "we need to speak with you now. Would you like to meet us at the gate, or should we come in?"

There was a long pause, a faint huffing sound like an exhale, and then the door in the hedge buzzed. Adele shrugged, glancing at John. Renee, who still had his hand raised from where he'd been miming a drink. He slowly lowered his hand, returning her expectant glance.

"Well then," John murmured. "He's definitely drunk."

"He's also scared," Adele added. "You heard his reaction at DGSI?" She trailed off as the speaker crackled to life again. But the man didn't say anything, suggesting perhaps he was just trying to listen in.

Shooting Renee a knowing glance, Adele moved up the garden path, walking swiftly across a cobblestone pathway with red- and green-stained bricks. Along the garden path, beds of redolent flowers complemented expensive statues of stone and bronze. One such bronze creation was of a full-sized horse in motion.

Even Adele, who wasn't fond of animals larger than humans, had to admit the artistry was beautiful.

But while rich people had their toys and expensive items, Adele couldn't afford to get distracted. She hastened forward along the path, marching toward the giant oak and glass double doors behind the three white pillars.

She thought she spotted movement in one of the first-floor windows, but when she looked, the only motion was of a disturbed curtain fluttering on the breeze. Adele picked up the pace, ignoring the feeling of the fresh bandages rubbing against her side.

Together, she and John stepped into the shadow of the enormous, high-ceilinged, two-story Parisian manor. The turret alone would have been intimidating enough, but the accompanying statuary and occasional ornamental pillar also left its impact.

Adele and John reached the door simultaneously. As they stepped up the marble stairs, a silhouette moved on the other side of a gap between the giant double doors. A large brass knocker shaped like an elephant's head shifted perceptibly as the door was pulled open from within.

Though it wasn't so much a pull as a shove.

The occupant of the French manor glared out at them with bleary, red-ringed eyes. He sniffed a couple of times, wiping at his upper lip with the back of his right hand. Even standing back a few paces, Adele could smell him. He clearly hadn't showered in a while, but the stench of sweat and oily clothing was secondary to the odor of alcohol coming from him in waves. He opened his mouth to speak, but ended up burping instead, adding reinforcements to his overall stench.

"You are feds?" he asked after he'd managed to hold back an impromptu upchuck. He held a fist to his mouth, as if sealing everything in.

"Are you Mr. Weeks?"

The man stepped closer to the gap in the door, emerging from the threshold of a grand hall behind him. A couple of decorative vases had been toppled recently, judging by the mangled flowers and spreading layer of water that went ignored. The crawling puddle reached the bottom step of an enormous stairwell.

The man in the door didn't seem to notice or mind.

"Are you alright?" John said, looking at one of the smashed vases. "Is anyone else in there?"

The man in the door hesitated. Burped again. Glanced back and then went still as one of his statues. After a few moments, though, his eyes suddenly widened. "Oh!" he exclaimed. "No—no, no. I did that. No one else is here. Yes, this is my home. I'm Anton Weeks. What about it? I haven't done anything wrong!" He said all of this in a jumble of rapidly spewed words. His eyes kept darting between the two agents as if trying to gauge the greater threat.

John pointed toward the vases. "Looks like you might want a towel or two."

Anton glanced back again. He frowned, then shook his head. "No, no… It's fine. I tripped."

"Twice?"

"Yes, twice."

"Over the same large item?" John asked. "Sir… I hate to ask this, but have you been taste-testing… anything alcoholic recently? Maybe something that comes in powdered form?"

The inference was lost on their suspect. The ex-owner of the defunct jewelry line shook his head. Adele couldn't help but notice the man wasn't wearing any jewelry himself. No bracelets, earrings, or even a watch. His wrists were bare. He also only barely resembled his driver's license photograph. The ill-shaved stubble and stringy dark hair over a too-large forehead might otherwise have obscured those sharp cheekbones, and the once playful eyes of a full-grown man who hadn't quite grown up.

Now, though, that spark that she'd seen in his online picture was gone. The youthful good looks of a jewelry brand CEO had vanished.

This was a man who'd spent the last year or so sulking and experimenting with harder and harder substances if her instincts were to be trusted.

"Sir," John said slowly, "do you mind if I step into your home?"

The man didn't even seem to register the question, no less put up protest. John, who'd never much needed express permission anyway, slipped past the bathrobe-wearing ex-CEO. Renee stepped over the spreading vase puddle, looking down at the pink and red petals from the broken flower stems.

Adele returned her attention to the man himself, indifferent to his manner at least for the moment. The man shifted uncomfortably under her scrutiny, seemingly interested very much in his shoelaces all of a sudden. These, Adele noticed, had been tied in a tangle of many knots as opposed to bows.

He just stared at his feet, seemingly fascinated.

"Sir, I need to ask you a few questions," Adele said slowly. "Are you able to answer coherently or do we need to call paramedics?"

He looked up, a panicked look in his eyes. "I'm not leaving! This is my home! You can't make me leave."

"My intention is not to make you do anything, sir. I just need to speak with you about your company. Sheen and Splendor—you owned the jewelry brand, yes?"

His eyes sparked at the mention of the brand's name. He gave a little childish giggle and sniffed once more, but this time didn't wipe at his face. Instead, he pointed both fingers at Adele.

"You're pretty," he said. "Ha! I used to have all sorts of pretty ladies in my store. Just like you."

"I believe you. But you closed down," Adele said, deciding to go on this fishing expedition slowly. The man was already confused, no sense in befuddling him further.

As she spoke, though, she was surprised to see tears suddenly form in his eyes. He nodded, letting loose a little sob. "Yes—yes! It's true," he said. "Oh dear... oh my... Where... where's the other one?" He was looking over his shoulder again, but John had slipped off into a side room, and Adele had lost track of her partner.

"What other one?" she said innocently.

The man frowned as if trying to remember something, but Adele cut in before he could. "I want to speak to you about an employee of yours. A woman—a clerk. She went missing the day before you closed down. I'm curious if anyone ever spoke to you about this."

He sniffed again, crossing his arms. "Of course we spoke," he said. "But... but at the time..." He gave a helpless little shrug and spread his hands, indicating the space around him. "I had a bit of say in things... I... well..."

"So they did speak to you, but you paid them to let it go?"

"What? No—no I didn't say..."

"Because if that's what you're implying," Adele pressed on like a train, refusing to slow down for even a second, "then it might very well imply, sir, that you had something to hide. Why bribe anyone? Why shut down your company?"

He was still crying at the thought of his lost jewelry line. But the more questions she asked, the more flustered he grew. Now that she repeated the question again, he was slowly leaning against the door frame and slipping down the wood. His robe snagged on one of the hinges, but this didn't deter his descent. He collapsed all at once, like a marionette with snipped strings.

He sat in a puddle from the shattered vase, but if he noticed the water seeping through his bathrobe, he gave no indication. He burped once more and leaned back against the doorjamb. Only then did he look up at her again, scratching at his chin bristles. "Oh, hi there!" he said cheerfully. "Am I expecting you?"

Adele felt a surge of frustration. Interviewing an inebriated suspect wouldn't be a very reliable testimony in court. But she wasn't trying to press charges in a court. She was trying to find out how Mr. Weeks was involved with all of this. A woman had gone missing at his store. Vanished. He'd then closed his jewelry line the day after. Now it sounded as if he'd bribed police not to look too closely.

And there, sitting in his puddle in his bathrobe, he was clearly upset by the line of questioning. Though in his state, she wouldn't have doubted most things might make him upset.

But if he had killed a woman before, who was to say he wasn't doing it again? Especially if they were wearing jewelry in his defunct line.

Adele tried a more aggressive approach now. "Sir, do you like it when you see women wearing your jewelry out in public? I can't help but notice you're not wearing anything."

"What?"

"You heard me. Answer my question, please. Do you like seeing your jewelry in public? Or... does it make you angry? Mad? Mad enough to make them take it off, perhaps? To do something about it?"

The man looked flabbergasted. He remained reclined against the doorjamb, but just kept shaking his head. "I don't know what you're saying," he murmured. "Do I know you?"

Adele's temper flared, but she resisted the urge to snap at him. As she opened her mouth to reply, however, Agent Renee's voice suddenly echoed out from down the hall. He had something in his hand, which he raised, waving toward them.

John sidestepped a cleaning trolley full of Windex and bleach and scrub brushes—the sort a cleaning lady might use—and ducked under a very low-hanging chandelier that someone had forgotten to raise again.

As he drew nearer, his footsteps rapidly tapping against the ground, Adele finally made out the item in his large palm.

A burner phone. In fact, the same brand of phone that had been used in the last two crime scenes.

Adele stared, feeling a sudden flash of excitement. John scowled, cuffs already emerging in his hands.

Adele shot a quick look toward the babbling idiot on the ground. She half expected to find him looking up at her, menacing and sober all of a sudden as if putting on a performance.

But he was just glancing at John, confused. "Who are you?"

"Is that one of the killer's phones?" Adele asked, ignoring Mr. Weeks.

John, in answer, snapped, "Anton Weeks, you're under arrest. Please rise to your feet, or I'll have to make you."

Mr. Weeks still looked confounded. But he was able, it seemed, to detect the note of fury in John's tone. He seemed sober enough to realize that something had changed, and that it had to do with the item in Renee's hand.

Mr. Weeks let out a faint sigh. He swirled a finger through the puddle beneath him. And then he pushed slowly to his feet, murmuring, "I never should have done it. I... she didn't deserve it. I'm sorry. I'm so, so sorry."

"You can save your apologies until we're back at the station," Adele said. "I'm sure there are a lot of people there who'd like to hear you."

Mr. Weeks hung his head, tears slipping down his cheeks. He looked miserable now. There was no sign of the mockery, the laughter, the teasing. No sign of the man who'd slipped past security cameras. Perhaps he once had been... perhaps even this morning, hours ago, before he'd drowned himself to stave off his guilt.

But now, the man they were handcuffing, the man they were guiding away from his home, down the garden path...

He was just a small, sad man.

The sort of man Adele might not have noticed in a crowd.

He was crying, but she couldn't help but wonder if they were crocodile tears. Was he sad because he'd killed those women? Or sad because he'd been caught?

They reached the gate in the hedge, and Adele's cheeks were prickling, her skin buzzing as John pushed Mr. Weeks through, toward the waiting car.

The enormous French manor rose up behind them, looming against the horizon. Adele glanced back, feeling a flicker of familiarity. Her old mentor, Robert Henry, had once lived in a similar home. Though not even Robert's place had been as big as this.

But the men had been two entirely different people.

Robert had been kind, sober, somber, professional. He'd been the sort to sacrifice his well-being for others. He'd even provided a home for Adele. She missed Robert. A serial killer had slain him in his own home to get at her.

She still carried those scars.

This man, though, Anton Weeks, didn't seem to have a spine. The idea of sacrificing one's own well-being for another's was likely a foreign concept for Mr. Weeks. The idea of taking a bath was similarly alien, or so she determined by his odor.

But one thing was certain; in Robert Henry's case, wealth had made him generous, open-handed...

But where Mr. Weeks was concerned, it had only amplified his worse traits.

And somehow all of it had led to murder.

Tears or not, he had to answer for his crimes.

CHAPTER TWENTY TWO

Adele was the one who'd requested the fan. Now, the small breeze was blowing the worst of Mr. Weeks's sweat, alcohol, and body odor stench away from her. She sat on one side of a small interrogation table in the largest room the police sergeant had available.

But it still wasn't big enough. Singed sinuses were a small price to pay for collaring a bad guy, though.

Adele's elbow brushed Renee's as the two of them finished scrolling through their notes on their phones.

John cleared his throat and spoke first.

"No arrest record," he said quietly. "No previous criminal charges. You've lived beneath the radar, Anton... So what happened?"

The rich man was still crying. He hadn't sobered up much in the drive over, but he had asked more than once who Adele and John were. And now, a similar look of confusion she'd seen in the rearview mirror displayed across his features.

"I'm Agent Sharp," Adele cut in, before he could ask. "And you are a murderer."

He blinked at this. "I... I... What?"

Adele sighed. This was about as much progress as they seemed able to make. No matter what she said or did, Mr. Weeks just didn't seem coherent enough to offer anything useful.

She was wondering if perhaps trying a different approach would be fruitful, or if they'd simply have to wait until he sobered up to have anything near a fruitful conversation.

"Sir," Adele said, "I need you to focus." She snapped her fingers over the table between them.

He blinked with each click. "Yes," he said. "Agent Sharp." He nodded at her.

"That's right," she replied. "What happened to Bernice Wallen? She was an employee, wasn't she? What about Lois Erfurt... Or Sofya Mere?"

But Mr. Weeks didn't even need to hear the names of his most recent victims. At the mention of Bernice, he looked as if he'd been slapped.

His face went pale as snow, and he tried to stammer a couple of times, but in the end just blinked and looked around as if he were lost. Clearly high, half-drunk, and barely coherent, this particular interrogation was going to feel like draining water from a rock. Adele let out a fluttering sigh of frustration, but composed herself and tried again. He'd reacted at Ms. Wallen's name.

His first victim? Perhaps just the first murder... There were often other types of victimization where serial killers were involved. They slowly escalated to murder.

Adele cleared her throat, regaining Mr. Weeks's attention, and she tried again. "Bernice," she said, as if the word itself were some type of button.

And it worked.

Again, Mr. Weeks's eyes flared. He let out a couple of panting breaths which culminated in a moan, and then his head fell, his oily hair draping toward the table. "Oh dear God," Anton declared, shaking his head and sniffing. "She... she was so kind... So nice. Everyone liked her. Some of us were even sweet on her. She didn't deserve... didn't deserve to..."

"To what?" John insisted. "What did you do to her?"

The agents both went quiet, leaning forward as if on tenterhooks. But Anton was off put by the sudden shift in intensity, and he glanced between them now from behind his fallen bangs. He huffed a couple of times in an effort to clear the hair from his eyes.

But failed both times.

Adele, taking the opportunity, pushed from her seat and sat on the edge of the table facing Anton. She reached out, brushing his hair from his eyes on his behalf. He stared up at her, like a child acknowledging his mother.

"What did you do, Anton?" Adele said quietly, having now postured herself elevated, but still seated in an attempt to communicate authority. She resisted the urge to wipe her hand on her thigh.

As she stared at the jewelry store owner, she couldn't help but feel a flash of anger. They'd found the same phone in his house as the ones used to taunt witnesses. Where was all his bravado now? Where was the mockery, the taunting? She'd often found with killers, much like online personalities, they were often full of bluster and brash up until the point they were confronted by someone who they didn't have power over.

Men like this, killers, were the weakest form of humanity. They took out their own insecurities on others. The cost of destroying things was nothing—just self-indulgence. Very similar to how this man clearly overindulged on narcotics and liquor. Learning to control one's impulses, one's self, was no easy task, and yet Adele had grown up in a household where this very thing had been something of a life mantra.

She couldn't help but feel, sitting on the table, staring at the man, that somehow he had reached the far end of a branching path.

And now he was blubbering in an interrogation room.

She often managed to conjure some sympathy, some pity for the men who killed. But now she simply stared, feeling only anger. It wasn't right that he'd taunted and heckled while safe in his mansion only to lose every bone in his spine the moment he sat down across from two agents.

"Sir," she tried again, struggling to keep his attention. "I need you to focus. What happened to your employee? What happened to Bernice Wallen? It was a year ago, sir. She went missing one year ago. And then you closed your store... you closed the jewelry line. Why?"

He sniffed. A teardrop hit the metal table between his arms. He murmured something.

"What was that?"

He coughed, and, in a rasping voice, louder, he said, "Phone... Please get my phone."

"Why? Sir, I need to know why before I'm allowed to—"

"Footage," he said quickly in that same haunted voice as before. "Camera footage—security cameras from that... that horrible day."

He looked at her now, his eyes stained red, his cheeks streaked with tears. His forehead was so greasy, unwashed as he was, that his sweat was leaving lighter trails across his skin.

John, who'd been the one to confiscate Mr. Weeks's phone, reached into his pocket, pulling out the two devices. "Which one?" he said. "Your personal phone or your little murder device?"

Weeks glanced between the two phones, blinking. He pointed at the burner. John began to extend it, but Weeks said, "I have no clue what that is. That's not mine."

"It was in your house," John said. "Hidden in your kitchen."

Weeks just blinked in confusion, but then shrugged as if this had to be true. He extended his fingers, though, clicking toward the second device John was holding. A sleek, dark smartphone covered in fingerprints and encased in a flowery protective shield.

"How about you tell me what the code is," John said gruffly. "I'm not about to give you the opportunity to delete anything."

Clearly, judging by Renee's tone, he wasn't buying the act either. Adele waited patiently, allowing her equally seasoned partner to navigate the exchange. Mr. Weeks blinked in surprise, but then snorted and shook his head. "Fine," he said. The password is... His voice choked. "Berni."

"With a y or an i?" John asked. "Or wait, an e?"

Mr. Weeks was glancing off again, as if he hadn't heard. John evidently tried all three, because after a glare then a grunt, his eyes suddenly brightened, and he lifted the phone. "I'm in... So what do you want to show us?"

The jewelry tycoon glanced back. He almost looked bored now. The tears had vanished. His eyes were hooded, and he yawned. "The footage! The footage, of course! I told you. Well, what do you think I meant? It's all there! All of it!" This mini outburst lulled, but then he continued suddenly, yelling now, spittle flecking across the table. "I did it! I know I should have... shouldn't have. Shit! Damn it. This day was coming. I knew it. I—I kept the footage. I should've... I know I should have done something when I... but there it is. See for yourself..."

He trailed off again.

John looked hesitant now. But Adele, doing her best to read between the lines of the mini rant, murmured, "Check saved videos from last year," she said.

John used a finger to scroll across the screen. A second later, he tensed.

"One video," he murmured.

Adele pushed off the table, circling it to rejoin him now. She frowned as she brushed against his shoulder, and the two of them peered at the image. It was grainy security footage of a doorway and sidewalk outside a storefront.

"Is this your shop?" Adele asked.

Mr. Weeks nodded glumly. "I'd never seen a body before," he whispered. "Not a... not a *dead* one."

Adele looked sharply at him. This was as close as he'd gotten to explicitly admitting his crime.

"What was that, sir?" she asked, hoping he'd speak louder and the mic in the camera above them would be sure to pick it up.

But he looked dazed now and again glanced off, staring away from the two agents.

Adele returned her attention to the security footage on Mr. Weeks's phone. The time stamp showed they were being treated to a display of early morning foot traffic at the start of the day...

The same day Ms. Wallen had gone missing.

And then, a second later, the jewelry store clerk appeared on the screen. Adele recognized her from the woman's driver's license photo. Even in the grainy footage, the woman seemed to have pep, a bounce in her step. She smiled and waved to someone out of frame walking the other direction.

And then she entered the store. The door shut slowly behind her.

Adele and John watched with bated breath, waiting expectantly. But nothing happened. John sped up the image, swiping his finger along the bar at the bottom while moving slowly enough they were able to watch a hyper-sped version of the footage.

But mostly, for two hours, nothing happened. Ms. Wallen must have arrived well before the store hours started, because no one else entered or exited the jewelry shop. This struck Adele as somewhat strange, but stranger still was how the footage ended.

About two hours after Ms. Wallen had arrived to work, the door suddenly swung open again.

But this time, it wasn't the clerk emerging.

Rather, Mr. Weeks, looking far more refined and *clean*, emerged stumbling from his own store, wearing a panicked look. Even in the poor image quality, it seemed clear he was crying. He had slick, gelled hair and a neat, Italian notched-cuff suit. He was hyperventilating and bent double, gasping at the ground.

For a moment, Adele thought he was going to throw up.

But then the small figure in the image stumbled away from the door to his shop. A moment later, he seemed to realize something and sprinted back toward the door. He kept shooting panicked, teary-eyed looks up and down the street. A pedestrian brushed past Mr. Weeks, but the store owner didn't even seem to notice. He was busy fumbling for keys with clearly trembling fingers.

Once he made sure to lock, then double and triple check the lock, to his business place, he stowed the keys, smoothed his hair, and did his best to compose himself before hurrying away again, this time in the exact opposite direction he'd been heading before.

And then the video footage ended.

They both looked up at their suspect, and Anton looked far calmer now than he had before. His hands were folded on the table in front of them, and his gaze didn't dart so much as spotlight; first John, then Adele.

"I have the rest of the footage on my computer back home," he said quietly, speaking coherently for the first time since they'd interacted. "It shows the same... She never leaves. She arrives, but she never leaves."

Adele stared back. "Why?" she said, her mouth dry all of a sudden.

Normally, it was much harder to get a killer to confess, but now Mr. Weeks was practically screaming his guilt.

Perhaps he really did have a tortured conscience like he was attempting to project. Or perhaps, now that he'd been caught, he was attempting to accrue as much sympathy as possible with his impending arrest and trial in mind.

With men like this, one could never tell.

Adele studied him now. "Why did she never leave the store?" Adele murmured. "Why?"

"I came back later," he replied stiffly. "But I use the alley entrance. I... I just didn't know what to do with the body."

"The body?" John snapped. "So you admit you killed her. What did you do to her body?" John glared across the table. "What did you do, you bastard!"

But Mr. Weeks was unperturbed by the harsh tone. He just let out a shaky, weary little sigh. Then he gave a faint shrug. "I..." he said softly. "I did what I had to. I... I needed to protect the business. Don't you understand? People were counting on me to keep them employed. I had business partners... had..." He let out another sob now, dipping his head. "I should have just called the police. I know that now. I wasn't able to keep the branch open. Not... not knowing what had happened. What I did." He swallowed a lump in his throat. "I couldn't take the guilt."

"So you closed your own business down... out of guilt?" Adele whispered. "So why kill the others? If you were so sad about killing your clerk, why murder again?"

He looked at her sharply now, eyes wide. "Kill? Wait, *what*? I didn't kill *her*! I found her like that."

"Who?" Adele said, feeling a sudden rush of discomfort. She felt as if they'd now reached the crescendo, the point of Mr. Weeks's act. Or was it an act? She watched him unblinking as he kept speaking.

"I found her body like that! Behind the counter. I had no clue what happened! I just couldn't—couldn't do anything to... I tried to save her! I really did. But she was dead. Strangled. I don't... I mean..." He choked, sobbing again. "All the blood. I don't know who would do something like that to a woman's hand. But all the blood, and I just... I slipped and then... shit. Changed pants. But look! I didn't kill her! I just was trying to do what was best for the company! That's all."

"You didn't *kill* Ms. Wallen," Adele said slowly, "but you were seen on video leaving the location where we, also on video, see her arrive.

112

Was anyone else at the store with you?" She didn't even try to keep the doubt from her tone.

He gave a miserable shake of his head. "No," he whispered. "The demons did it. I—I never believed before. But it was the only way. The demons must have done it. The jewelry was cursed. I had to close it all down. I couldn't keep sending that cursed stuff to clients! Not after what happened to Bernice."

John just snorted, shaking his head in sheer derision. Adele sighed, biting her bottom lip to hold back what she thought of this ploy.

The demons did it...

She'd met some very odd murderers in her time, but no one had used *demons* as their attempt of an alibi. "Sir," she said quietly, "I don't believe you're as clever as you think you are." She glared at him. Normally, she wasn't one to reprimand killers. Especially ones who had provided material evidence of their own crimes. But she just couldn't forget that voice on the phone. The jeering... the sheer *fun* the bastard seemed to have at the thought of ending women's lives. And now there he sat, mocking them still. A different type of mockery, but still the same substance.

She pointed at him. "You admit to disposing of your victim's body, then?"

He nodded miserably. "I didn't kill her... I just hid her... I worked so hard to start Sheen and Splendor. I couldn't imagine what a corpse in a high-end jewelers would do to the sales! Don't you see... I had to. For... for the sake of the brand. People in this business are cut-throat. Don't even get me started on the news outlets that cover us. Worse than gossip columns."

"So you murder a woman and hide her body?" John insisted.

"No! No! I didn't kill her. I hid her. That's it! I cleaned up the blood. I wanted it to be as if nothing had ever happened... No one knew... Except me. And the demons."

"And these demons," John said slowly. "They make a habit of speaking with you?"

"No—no, I don't hear them. They killed Berni, though. Killed her in my store." He let out a rattling breath and shrugged. His form suddenly slumped in his chair, and he lowered his head to rest it against the back of his knuckles.

Adele shot John a look. He gave an exasperated sigh. It felt like a ball bearing circling a drain, but never quite falling through. Mr. Weeks was confessing... but not quite. Maybe that was his play. A hope to get indicted on *lesser* charges to avoid a murder sentence.

But this tactic wasn't an unfamiliar one. Suspects often thought that by camouflaging their true actions by confessing to smaller crimes, they'd deflect police scrutiny.

But it wouldn't work. Certainly not with Adele on his case.

She shot John a look, and the big man gave a brief nod.

She wondered if he was thinking the same thing. A second later, though, they both turned to Mr. Weeks. There seemed an obvious next step. One that Anton had spoon fed them.

Simultaneously, John and Adele both spoke. "Where'd you hide the body?"

Weeks didn't say anything now. He remained with his head bowed, his shoulders shaking. Adele tried again. "Sir, if what you're saying is true, we need to know where you hid Ms. Wallen."

He didn't reply. He didn't even act as if he'd registered the question.

Adele frowned, watching the shaking man. She'd seen the footage too, though. By his own admission, Ms. Wallen went in then never reemerged.

Which meant there was only one potential location for the corpse.

A body buried for a year wouldn't be the perfect witness... but all crime scenes told tales. Even months later.

They needed to visit the location of the jewelry store. They needed to find Ms. Wallen's body. Then no amount of tall tales or redirection would help their killer.

Bodies didn't lie. Only people did.

Besides, it didn't look as if further conversation with Anton at this point would yield much fruit. If Adele remembered correctly, the old jewelry store location wasn't far from the precinct. She tapped John on the shoulder and nodded toward the door.

He gave a quick thumbs-up, leaned in, and murmured, "Need a cop on this guy. Suicide watch."

Adele nodded, already moving toward the door to fetch a babysitter, while she reached into her pocket to pull out her phone and locate the address of the brick and mortar location of Sheen and Splendor.

One way or another, they would find that body.

CHAPTER TWENTY THREE

Adele wrinkled her nose, doing her best not to inhale concrete dust. She watched, her expression grim, as the three diggers lowered the jack hammer and giant chisel they'd been using to tear up the abandoned store's concrete floors.

She waved a hand to clear the dust once more. Agent Renee was helping the diggers, merrily swinging the hammer into the chisel as if it had personally insulted him. She spared only a glance at John, admiring the way his muscles rippled, his chest straining against his T-shirt. His suit and outer layer were draped over a counter on the other side of the room.

Save this marble protrusion from the floor, the space was now bare. No reminder of the many glistening and valuable trinkets once displayed. No reminder of the woman who'd been killed here, either.

And now, staring at the gap in the floor, Adele's fears were confirmed. The digging crew had located freshly poured cement that didn't quite match the rest of the ground.

After nearly a half hour of effort, coordination, and ventilation so they didn't all choke on concrete powder, their labor was paying off.

The payment, though, was a grim one.

John reacted first, cursing and gripping the foreman's arm, holding him back. The two other workers went still a second later. All of them stared into the dark hole.

Adele tentatively joined them. A coroner, whom they'd also called, lingering next to her, stepped forward as well.

The six of them, holding hands to their faces in an attempt to filter out the air, leaned in, staring into the dark crevice under the concrete.

They all had spotted the body.

Thin bones, emaciated, with stained clothing—gaping, skeletal eyes staring up at them with an accusing leer. Adele noticed immediately that one of the hands was missing. The rest of the body looked intact.

Carefully, following the coroner's quick instructions, the diggers looped a fabric swing beneath the corpse on either side. A stretcher beneath a plastic tarp was hastily placed as near to the hole as possible.

For this part, John and Adele retreated a few steps, watching with equally somber expressions.

"He led us right to it," John murmured, his voice muffled from where he kept his hand cupped over his lips.

Adele could taste concrete on her tongue, and she glanced back at the glass door, making sure it was still propped open by the cinderblock.

"I know," she murmured. "I still don't know what his game is."

John snorted. "Lighter sentence. Cooperating with authorities."

Adele shrugged, nodded. She was starting to feel a sense of discomfort that she didn't want to share with Renee. Mostly because she didn't want to upset him.

But part of her was now wondering if they'd missed something. She watched absentmindedly as the body was lifted onto the stretcher. Bits and pieces of dust and concrete scattered, falling in a shower back into the hole in the ground.

For a year, the body had been hidden beneath the floor. If, indeed, it really was Ms. Wallen.

"Make sure to look for others!" Adele called out. "There might be more corpses!"

The foreman gave a sigh, but then nodded. He handed a flashlight to the youngest digger and muttered a few instructions. The corpse was shifted off to the side, where the coroner, wearing protective gloves, gave a cursory inspection.

Adele's eyes darted from the diggers to the coroner, trying to keep track of their movements.

She wasn't sure what the next step was.

The killer was in custody. Now it was all about building a case.

The flashlight beam disappeared as the digger dropped into the crawl space where the body had been. Adele didn't envy him the task. The coroner was holding something up so they could see. A wallet. She'd pulled out an ID and called out, "Bernice Wallen!"

Adele sighed, nodding back.

So far, everything was playing out exactly how Anton had told them it would.

Which only left one question.

Why the hell had he told them?

Why had he kept that security footage on his phone? Why had he kept that burner phone in a place easy enough for John to discover?

Adele very much wanted to tie this all off with a bow and go on her merry way, reporting a success back to Foucault.

But she also knew that her mind didn't work like that.

She needed the *truth*. Not her version of it. Not the easy out.

And there were still so many unanswered questions. She watched as a flashlight beam appeared again, and a face emerged. "Nothing else!" the figure called, shaking his head.

Adele stepped forward. "No other bodies?" she asked.

The figure, hastily clambering out of the hole in the concrete, still shook his head. Adele hesitated, but then extended a hand. "Mind if I?"

The young man was more than willing to hand off the flashlight. Adele accepted it with a grateful nod. Then, tensed, breathing in shallow puffs, she approached the dark crater. Her eyes darted briefly toward the body with the coroner.

The left hand was clearly missing. No sign of it on the tarp, either.

Adele shivered. Just like the other victims—a severed appendage. This was where it all had started. The first murder, no doubt. A murder that he'd covered up in concrete, hiding it beneath his own floors.

She ducked beneath the crawlspace, holding her breath and lifting the flashlight.

She shifted from one foot to the next, chips of concrete textured like gravel crunching beneath her shoes. She shone the light across the small space beneath the floor. First checking one dusty corner, then the next.

There wasn't much room. Only enough to crouch, or lie down. And there wasn't much in the way of debris, either, save what had been created by the crew she'd brought.

Something else was missing, though…

The digger had been right. No other bodies. No corpses… But this wasn't what caught her attention.

She frowned, flashing the light once more. Trying not to think that she was now inhaling air that had only known a rotting corpse for a year.

She felt shivers along her arms and tried to push the thought from her mind, still rotating like a lighthouse. Spotlighting one way, then the other. She let out a faint puff of air, feeling the prickle spread to her cheeks.

It wasn't here.

How did that make sense?

Why wasn't it here?

She gave a final, slow sweep of the space beneath the floor, but realized her initial assessment was correct.

It wasn't here.

So where was it?

She frowned, grateful to rise out of the hole once more. Agent

Renee extended a hand which she accepted, pulling herself from the crawlspace.

"Nothing?" John said.

She shook her head. The young digger looked relieved.

Adele said, "Absolutely nothing."

John furrowed his brow. The diggers were packing up their gear, tending to the jackhammer. The coroner was busy jotting down some notes on her phone.

"John…" Adele said, "Mr. Weeks mentioned blood, yes? Everywhere."

John pointed toward the corpse. "Missing hand," he said.

"Exactly! Missing. So where is it? We found the body… where's the hand?"

John hesitated. "I—well… You're sure it isn't down there?"

"Perfectly sure. Nothing else is down there."

"Hmm. Maybe Weeks took it with him."

Adele shook her head. "We saw the camera footage. He wasn't carrying anything. Plus, did he seem in the emotional state to lug around a bloody stump?"

John bit his lip. "I… maybe later. He said he returned through a side door."

Adele huffed. "Yes… yes, possibly. It would have taken time to do all this," she said, waving toward the floor. "But… but why *take* the hand? Why not just bury it with the rest of the body?"

John shook his head. "The other victims' body parts were found distant from the rest of their corpses. Maybe it's some sick MO. Who knows how these guys think."

"We do. At least, we're supposed to know. And John… I don't see how one moment that man is stumbling from his own shop, weeping and snotty, and the next he's walking away with a murder victim's severed hand."

"He did it before."

"No, he never took the body parts with him!" she insisted. "He left them."

"Well… maybe it's here somewhere?" John leaned over, looking behind the only counter in the place.

"Where?" Adele asked, spreading her hands. "There's nowhere *to* hide it."

John shrugged. "We can't answer *every* question, Adele. Frankly, I'm not sure it matters. We have our guy. That's good enough, isn't it?"

Adele allowed the silence to linger. She wasn't sure what else there

118

was to say. John was right, in a way.

They *did* have their guy.

So why was she still so uncertain?

The answer, of course, was obvious. Did she really think Anton was capable of the murders on the trains? The mind displayed there had been a cold, clever, calculating one. The man they'd interrogated had been hopped up on pills and drink…

Unless he'd just been acting.

But if so, why had he shown them footage? Why had he led them to his own victim? No one had found this particular body. Not in a year.

Had he simply panicked?

She nibbled at the corner of her lip, trying to think clearly. John scowled, though, letting out a sigh. "Shit," he said.

"What?"

"That look on your face."

"What look?"

"That look you get when you want to kick over more stones. Stop kicking, Adele. This is it. We don't have to know every detail of a psycho's plan. We got him. He admitted to killing her. To burying her."

"No! He admitted to hiding a body. Not to killing her."

John snorted. "In a closed room with no one else around, by his own testimony."

"Unless," she murmured, "he missed someone. I'm not saying he didn't do it. I'm just saying we need all the information we can get."

John closed his eyes and rubbed at his face.

Adele pointed to one side. "That looks like it might have once been an office space before the wall was knocked down. What if Mr. Weeks wasn't actually *in* this room with the clerk?" She pointed toward the metal side door that led into an alley. "Anton himself said he used that door to return. What if someone *else* who knew about the cameras avoided them by coming this way?"

John just gaped at her. "You seriously believe this guy? He's mental, Adele. He blamed demons."

"He was drunk and high. But you may be right… I just… just…"

"Just what?"

She sighed, lip curling as she tasted more dust on her tongue. "Just want to check into the murder case from last year. To see if there's anything else we're missing around the time of Ms. Wallen's death."

"And how do you plan to do that?"

Adele shrugged. "I mean… he's been a pretty reliable source so far." She waved a hand to the body.

119

John grunted. "You wanna talk to that loony bin again?"

"Couldn't hurt. Besides, if I'm wrong, which I probably am, a little due diligence wouldn't hurt. He might admit to other murders. He's not exactly versed in self-preservation."

John ran a hand through his hair, dislodging a shower of dust. "Fine," he said at last. "I know you well enough not to get in the way. But... Do you need me with, or can I stick around and see what the coroner finds?"

"No, that's fine," Adele said quickly. "I'm sure it's nothing."

John gave her a grateful pat on the shoulder, and Adele turned, gliding up the floor and hastening back toward the front door.

She wasn't looking forward to another round with Mr. Weeks. But hopefully he'd sobered a bit. John was probably right. Everything pointed to Anton being their guy.

At least... *nearly* everything.

But where was the hand? Why had he led them to the body? Could a man like *that* really have orchestrated all these kills?

This time, as Adele pushed through the open door, sidestepping the cinderblock, she was determined that if he didn't give them willingly, she'd have to demand the answers she needed.

CHAPTER TWENTY FOUR

He wasn't smiling now... He wanted to, but this was always the hardest part. Finding the perfect match. True love, of course, couldn't be rushed.

He sat in the plastic seat, back straight, eyes ahead. Every so often, though, he shot a glance one way, then the other. Eyes darting from women's necks to ankles to wrists, to ears... Anywhere he might find *them*. Those same little pieces of hell. The jewelry she had chosen over him.

A career. That's what she'd called it.

A damn career.

Well... he'd seen to that little disagreement. Things had escalated. She'd called herself Mr. Weeks's right-hand lady.

Just a little fun he'd left her with *only* her right hand. Besides, her left had carried the small engagement ring he'd been able to afford at the time.

Those things, especially from such a damn racket as Sheen and Splendor, hadn't come cheap. Bernice had never been cheap, either.

His grip tightened on the yellow bar leading from the floor to the ceiling. He held tight as the train jounced along the tracks.

As he glanced at the other passengers though, searching for the perfect match, he found it more difficult than ever. He had an eye for the ivy patterns and high carat stones. For two years he'd visited Bernice at her job, courting her. They'd been in love.

At least, he'd been in love, and he'd been willing to wait.

He wasn't much if not a patient man.

A good man. A man who had wanted to provide and love. Simple as that.

But she'd led him on. She'd kept him trapped for two years, lying to him... And then she'd chosen a career path over their true love.

He'd lost his temper. The rest was history.

He hadn't found out until months later that the jewelry store had closed down. This seemed fitting, like the end to a good play.

But it had also angered him. The jewelry store had cost him his lover. It had no right to up and *die*. Not without suffering like he had. No... no, but now those who'd participated in stealing her from him were getting their comeuppance.

He was making them pay. Trinkets and baubles instead of true love—it was enough to make a man go mad.

He pushed angrily from his plastic chair, still searching for any sign of the devilish little baubles. But the passengers in this train weren't hated foes. Weren't customers of the very place that had killed his true love.

Because, after all, the jewelry store was the real culprit behind Berni's death.

He had just struck the blow to end it all.

He shifted as the train came to a slow, scraping halt.

A few passengers started gathering their things, folding books or removing earbuds. He darted through the sliding doors first, hitting the platform and moving hastily toward one of the restrooms. He turned down a hall of the aboveground station. Behind him, he heard footsteps as other pedestrians disembarked.

A few passengers lingered in the station, waiting for commuters or watching their phones while likely planning itineraries. But even these folk didn't wear the right markers…

Perhaps he'd done it… Managed to stamp out completely those who had led to Berni's death.

He frowned.

A faint urge swirled in his gut, a longing. He'd already tasted *true* love. And he'd been rejected. She'd chosen her fate. As did all of them.

He'd once heard the question, would he rather be feared or loved.

It was a trick question.

It wasn't about what *he* wanted. But if love wasn't an option, by default, only fear remained…

And it tasted *almost* as good as what he'd once had with Bernice.

He looked around the train station, pretending he was getting something from a vending machine. The police were asking more questions, following him along the train lines. He wouldn't be as bold as he'd once been. But he would outsmart them.

He studied figures approaching in the reflection in the glass. A woman pushed into the restroom. A man took the stairs in the back, heading toward an office compartment.

He slipped a hand into his pocket, fingers grazing the metal found within. He frowned as he turned, his back against the cool glass.

If one of them wouldn't volunteer, if a match couldn't be found, perhaps he needed to find another way. That was it. He nodded to himself, his hair shifting against the glass. Yes, he'd let them self-select. It was only fair, after all.

After what they'd done to him. What they'd taken from him with their greed, with their jackdaw lust for all things sparkly.

So now he'd see which of them *wanted* to be chosen.

He pulled his hand from his pocket, this time emerging with an item… He stared at it briefly, a familiar longing rising in his gut.

He'd taken it from the hand he'd removed. Emeralds dotting curling, ornamental silver leaves. He held his hand up to his nose, as if inhaling the cold metal and glassy stones.

He wet his lip and allowed a faint smile.

Then, gently, he lowered the bracelet to the ground. It pooled like a snake coiling. He tried to walk away, but it took some doing. His head simply didn't want to leave it behind. But after a faint exhalation, and a summoning of inner strength, he pushed off his heel, his shoes squeaking faintly against the freshly mopped floor as he walked away from Bernice's old bracelet.

He reached the stairs, glanced up. No sign of movement. So he settled in his spot, eyes hooded, staring toward the vending machine and his little gift…

A poison gift.

The woman who'd used the restroom emerged first. She hastened past the vending machine without so much as a glance toward the floor, her eyes glued on her phone screen.

She chose her fate through ignorance. But he would respect the match.

The man returned next, moving back down the stairs. He shot a glance toward the stranger in the stairwell, but didn't say a word.

The man moved back up the hall, past the vending machine…

Then paused.

He frowned, glancing at the ground. His eyes widened suddenly, and he tensed. The fellow began to stoop, chuckling to himself as he reached for—

"Not yours," snapped the watcher in the stairwell.

The office man looked up sharply, eyes wide. He blinked, glanced toward the item on the floor, then frowned as if ready to protest.

"Alright then," whispered the watcher in the doorway. "Pick it up. See what happens."

The office man's protest died on his lips. He stared at the watcher, briefly frozen. Then, he muttered an insult and turned on his heel, doubling his pace as he hastened away.

The watcher smiled after the retreating form.

Better to be feared or loved?

The choice was getting easier and easier the more he went down this chosen path.

And that's when fate aligned.

She emerged.

His jaw fell, and his eyes threatened to pop.

A gorgeous, long-legged, beautiful creature. A brunette with curling hair and caramel skin. Her legs barely grazed as she practically floated down the hall. She paused by the vending machine, eyeing one of the small snack packs near the top.

The beautiful, leggy thing wasn't noticing the bracelet.

Shit.

She wasn't looking.

The watcher gritted his teeth, his heart pounding, feeling a flush of frustration. She started inserting a card into the machine's reader. So he hissed, waving. He pointed.

She glanced in his direction. Her face matched the rest of her— flawless. True love. Had he found it again?

But no... no, she first had to pick it up...

He nodded at her then bounced his eyes toward the ground. She stared at him, scandalized.

"No, no," he said quickly. "Not that... Look!"

Briefly, he felt a flicker of discomfort. Was he breaking the rules to his own game by directing her? Did it really matter? She was just too pretty to pass up.

The woman finally seemed to realize what he was indicating. Her eyes widened, and she slowly lowered, her fingers touching the bracelet. Her expression flickered in confusion, and she glanced back at him. But he was just smiling congenially in the threshold.

It was nice to smile again. He'd found a match.

What was there to be sad about?

Hesitantly, she ignored the snack pack which had tumbled from a curling spring-shaped wire. Her eyes were glued to the glinting bauble. Just like all of them. Like Bernice. The beautiful woman plucked the item off the ground and promptly looked away from him, as if worried he might stake a claim as well.

She began hurrying away, back in the direction she'd come from.

He watched her leave, smirking and enjoying the sight. And then, as she turned down the end of the hall, he began to follow, his pace quickening along with the drumming of his heart.

She'd chosen her fate. He might have helped a bit.

But she'd chosen.
She would have to be next.
The demands of love were steep, but worth it.
He smiled wider as he hastened down the hall in pursuit.

CHAPTER TWENTY FIVE

Adele paced up and down the hall outside the holding cell. She kept shooting glances toward where Mr. Weeks sat moaning on his cot. He'd refused to leave the cell. A few officers would have helped him exit, but Adele had decided against it.

And now she watched, studying him through the gray bars.

He held his head in his hands, still moaning. She'd even stopped by the desk sergeant's post, looking at the security footage over the last two hours.

His posture had never changed. If it was an act, it was a very good one.

She didn't speak at first, and he didn't seem to care, or even notice her. The air inside the holding unit was chill. The thick, bulletproof steel door behind her was sealed, locking her in with their suspect.

Not just any suspect, a prime suspect who'd practically confessed to the murders...

Except he hadn't... not fully.

He'd confessed to hiding a body. And then he'd broken down in front of her. Clearly, something was eating at his conscience.

He'd blamed demons, of all things, for killing his clerk.

Demons, Adele had decided, would be placed closer to the bottom of the list of suspects.

She considered her options, trying desperately to approach it from an angle that would *help*. Last time she'd spoken with him, she'd treated him like a suspect, because that was what he was... And it had yielded fruit. They'd found Bernice's body. Had found the hiding spot beneath the floor...

He'd clammed up since then, though.

So what if...

She considered this tactic, running through potential outcomes. But she then bobbed her head once, more for herself than for Mr. Weeks.

What if she didn't treat him like a suspect... what if she considered this a witness interview? The approach would be different. She wasn't here for corroboration alone. She wanted answers.

This decided, Adele cleared her throat.

He didn't blink.

She said, crisply, "Is there anything I can get you, sir?"

His head still hung in his hands. He didn't move.

She tried again. "Something to drink? Eat?"

He gave a moping shake, barely a twitch. He remained staring at the floor.

She sighed faintly. "I understand," she said. "Thank you for your cooperation. We found her, by the way. She was exactly where you told us."

He looked at her now, bleary-eyed, his eyelids puffy from crying. "You found her?"

And there it was again. A reaction at Bernice. Almost as if... as if...

"Sir," Adele said faintly. "Did you love her?"

He stared at her. "I... what?"

"Bernice Wallen. She seemed a very kind woman. She had kind eyes. I take it you cared for her."

He watched her through the bars, his brow furrowing. "You think I killed her," he said, his voice shaking with the accusation. "How can you think I killed her, if you know I loved her."

Adele nodded. "So you did?"

"She... she wasn't like anyone I'd ever met." He glanced off, his fingers running through his long hair. "She... she understood the art. Understood the point of it all. Each piece, perfectly suited for displaying some unique combination of both nature and geology and femininity. It was art, and she loved it. I loved her, yes... And I buried her." He sobbed again.

"You didn't kill her though?" This time, Adele said it gently, summoning what empathy she could find. Witness, not suspect. Witness, she kept reminding herself.

He snorted. "No! I've said as much. I did not kill her. I never would have. I found her dead. It broke me... but... but she loved the jewelry as much as I did. She and I made plans of going into business together. A partnership. She was going to leave her boyfriend for me. I... I was married to the job, but had finally found someone I could have seen myself—"

"Sir, I don't mean to interrupt. Thank you again. But if you found her body, why didn't you call the police?"

"I told you!" he exclaimed. "She was dead. Her bloody hand was missing. And...and it was what I'd been working for. What she'd been working for." His voice rose in volume now, and Adele wasn't sure if he was trying to convince her or himself.

Judging by the way his throat shook with guilt, though, it wasn't working on either of them.

"She would have wanted me to, yes, yes," he said quickly. His eyes turned to her again, wide and staring. "In our business, Agent Sharp, reputation is all that matters. Business was booming. I didn't need the scandal to ruin everything. Didn't need... indiscretions to come out."

"You were sleeping with her?"

He ignored this question. "I made the choice... And it lasted for a day. Less than that... But-but I couldn't bear the thought of doing it without her. She'd been there almost at the start, you know. I'd fallen instantly. The idea of going on... after what I'd done... Jamming her in that floor like some piece of junk." He shook his head. "I couldn't do it. I shut everything down. Sold the rest of our inventory to a competitor. It all died with her. Don't you see?"

Adele tucked her tongue inside her cheek, considering his words. Considering the desperation in his voice. She wasn't sure if she believed him or not. But *he* certainly seemed to believe what he was saying.

At the very least, he'd convinced himself.

"And these demons?" she said.

"What else could have done it?" he replied. "You saw the footage. No one else came or left."

"What about the side door?" Adele pressed.

He frowned. "Only Bernice and I had a key for that."

Adele's pulse quickened. She considered his words from earlier, eyes darting down to the ground, studying the floor if only to have something rigid to gaze on.

She looked up suddenly. "What about Ms. Wallen's boyfriend? You mentioned him twice. Did he have a key?"

"I... Oh, Timothe? No—no, of course not." He waved the thought away with a dismissive flick of his wrist.

Adele frowned, though. "Might he have had access to Bernice's key?"

Mr. Weeks stopped now, staring through the bars. "I... I don't know. I never talked to Berni about him. Why would I? She was going to leave him anyway!"

"Exactly," Adele said. The prickle had now spread from her arms to her fingers. She jammed a hand into her pocket, pulling out her phone. "Thank you, Mr. Weeks, for your time."

She turned, phone in hand, hastening back toward the sealed door and gesturing for the guard beyond to buzz it open.

As she moved, Mr. Weeks called after her. But she couldn't quite comprehend his words, her own mind spinning too quickly.

A jilted boyfriend, a woman with access to a key for a side door. A killer who'd made a habit of avoiding security cameras...

And also... A simple ask. Just a quick question. The hand was missing. Was something else also missing?

She lifted her device, waiting for the answer.

"Adele?" John's gruff voice came.

"Are you still there?"

"Hi to you, too. How's our walking pharmacy?"

"He's fine. Are you still there?"

"Yes. We're cleaning up. Tricky thing moving the body through the door. Coroner's assistants are trying to back their van up the curb."

"That's fine, John. Is the coroner still there?"

"Y-yes. Is everything okay, Adele?"

"Fine," she said quickly. "I need you to ask the coroner something."

"Alright. Shoot."

"John, ask her if she found any key on Ms. Wallen."

"A key?"

"Not a car key, nor an apartment key. Find all the keys she had and try them on the back door."

"Try them on—Adele, what's this about?"

"Please, John. Could you do it? No time."

As she said it, Adele realized her pulse was racing. She nodded a quick thank-you to the guard who buzzed her through the door, but kept moving, picking up her pace and taking long strides down the hall, toward the exit.

John sighed, but a few moments later she heard muffled speech. A pause. More speech. Adele could practically see the red tape swirling around her phone. John responded with a sharp comment. Adele winced.

But then she heard more heavy breathing. The sound of a rattle. A pause. More movement.

"John?" she tried.

Another few seconds passed. She heard a grunt. More rattling. And then a voice.

"Adele? Yeah—tried the keys. One looks like a car key. Another for an apartment. That's it. Neither fits the lock on this door."

Adele felt her heart quicken. "Bernice's key is missing," she murmured.

"What's that?"

"She had a key to the side door," Adele said quickly. "That's what

Mr. Weeks told me. Both of them had keys."

"Consider that he might be lying?"

"No—no, he didn't even suggest it. He brushed off the idea that anyone *else*..." She trailed off. If they had the wrong man behind bars, that meant the actual killer was still out there somewhere.

Still hunting.

She felt another surge of prickles, a chill, moving down her spine.

"John," she said urgently. "I have to hang up. I need to call the office."

"Adele, calm down. It's probably nothing. Whatever you're thinking, remember you're injured. Alright? Be safe. I'm coming to you."

"Fine. Thanks. See you."

She hung up. Her curt words weren't out of a lack of gratitude for Renee's help. Though she was starting to wish he wouldn't think of her as *injured.* Her side had barely throbbed once in the last hour. Though perhaps it was all the coffee she'd taken from the break room while watching the footage of the holding cell.

But no... no, she needed to locate Bernice's boyfriend. Shit. She needed a name.

She spun back, running now. The guard by the sealed door glanced up, eyes wide in surprise. She gestured toward him. "Open, please!" she said quickly. "Hurry."

He did. The door buzzed. She didn't stop to explain, but rather shouldered into the same holding cell hall again and hastened toward the crumpled form of Mr. Weeks. He was lying on his cot now, holding his legs up against his chest.

"Sir!" she called. "Anton, please, really quick, what was the name of Bernice's boyfriend?"

He moaned, one arm flopping over the edge of the bed.

"You come here to rub it in? Why ask me that? I've already suffered enough," he said.

Adele tried to keep her tone gentle, but it was difficult. "Sir," she said, more insistently. "Please. Focus. What was the name of the man who was dating her? Berni. That's what you called her, yes? I'm sure you loved her. So if you did, if..." Adele felt a flash of inspiration. "If you want to clear your conscience of what you did, help me now. Help Berni get justice."

He blinked, looking at her. "You... you think Timothe had something to do with it? Not... not demons?"

"Timothe—that's right. What's his last name?" Adele insisted.

"Please. Help me help her." She was breathing heavily now, one hand out, gripping the bars. The cold metal was rigid, refusing any give. She just stared at Mr. Weeks, desperately willing him to speak.

And then, with another moan and dramatic flop of his head, he said, "Vernier. His name is Timothe Vernier. And he's an asshole."

"Thank you!" Adele yelled. She turned, racing back down the hall, picking up the pace with each hurried step.

She was already placing another call. A name would lead to a phone number. A phone number would lead to a person.

Maybe she was wrong. Maybe Mr. Weeks was playing her for a fool. If so, then the only thing at stake was her reputation. And what did that matter in the face of catching a killer?

Mr. Weeks was behind bars. He would stay there until she said otherwise.

But if he was telling the truth...

The missing hand. The missing key. The admittance of hiding the body. The strange dichotomy between Anton's personality and the killer's...

There was every chance he was still out there. And judging by the rate he'd killed up to this point, she very well could already be too late to prevent another murder.

"Come on, come on," she muttered as her phone tried to connect.

And then a voice. "Agent Sharp?"

"Yes! Yes, Sami, I need you to run a number for me. Can you do that? Wait—no, hold on. I need you to find a number. Then run it."

The techie sounded almost bored by the job. "Name?" he said. She heard the clacking of keys.

Adele bit her lip, exhaling briefly. She shot a look back toward the sealed door to the holding cells. Was she being played?

But no... no, it didn't matter.

"Timothe Vernier," she said. "Hurry, please. Find where he is—track his phone. He might be on the move. If he is, tell me if he's anywhere near a train station. Hurry, please!"

The urgency in her tone was met by an increased flurry of typing. Sami said, "On it," sounding a little less bored all of a sudden.

Adele was already hastening back out of the hall, past the sergeant's desk and toward the exit. She prayed she was wrong, that she was just being tricked.

But part of her, now more than minutes before, felt certain that Vernier's phone would be located near a train station somewhere.

She could only hope when she arrived she'd find a survivor... and

131

not another victim.

CHAPTER TWENTY SIX

Adele cursed as she nearly slammed into the back of a slow-moving taxi. She shot a glance toward where her phone rested on the seat next to her. She listened as the speaker crackled, and Agent Sami's voice spoke. "It keeps fading in and out," Sami said, speaking louder so Adele could hear him over the sound of traffic. "But you're right on him."

Adele gritted her teeth, peering at the car in front of her. The taxi was driven by an old, gray-haired man who was humming along with some radio song Adele wasn't privy too.

"And the train line comes up when?" she shouted, veering back into the fast lane, in front of the taxi. Her tires squealed. Someone leaned on their horn. A glance in the rearview mirror told her the old taxi driver was still humming merrily along, indifferent to the flow of automobiles around him.

She slapped a hand against the steering wheel. "Come on, Sami. Are you sure you have the right number?"

It had occurred to her, with a horrible realization, that the killer might not have a regular phone. He kept more than his share of burners on hand. But Sami had confirmed the phone had been purchased nearly four years ago. The number had yet to be disconnected.

Which meant the killer had a personal phone but used the burners when he was out on the hunt. Now, they were tracking him by the GPS system on his device, thanks to an ingenious little trick of the DGSI tech agent.

"I told you," Sami said patiently, "he's on that train. You're keeping pace now. He'll arrive at the station two miles ahead."

Adele bit her lip, putting on an extra burst of speed and hastening toward the underground station indicated by a blue sign over a curling off-ramp. She took the ramp, hastening up the incline, her heart still somewhere in her throat.

"Come on, come on," she muttered beneath her breath.

The killer was on a train. Which meant he'd either struck again or he was hunting at that very moment. But this time... this time *she* had the advantage.

She knew his name. Timothe Vernier. She knew his connection to the first victim. Knew his connection the jewelry line. If ever there was a chance to catch him in time, this was it.

Her car squealed up the ramp, leaving rubber on the asphalt. She blew through a red light, blaring her horn to clear the way. She hit the sirens on the unmarked sedan. Blue and red lights flashed; the siren wailed as she blazed up the street, racing in the direction of the underground station, following Agent Sami's instructions over the phone.

"He's slowing!" Sami was saying. "He... lost him. Wait—no... He's beneath you. Right now. Are you almost there?"

Adele jumped a curb, moving over two lanes of traffic before pulling into the train station's parking lot. An attendant in a white booth just stared at her, slack-jawed, a cigarette threatening to tumble from between his lips.

She hit the siren, but left the lights going as an indicator for the backup Sami had already called in. The car's front door slammed behind her, and Adele took the stairs three at a time as she hurtled into the underground station.

Ahead, on the tracks, she heard the scraping sound of metal catching metal. The train screeched to a halt just as she reached the platform. Adele stumbled against a support column, one hand outstretched to halt her momentum.

Agent Renee wasn't here yet. She glanced quickly at her phone. Two missed calls. But he was on his way. She didn't have time to speak.

"Sami," she said hurriedly. "Where is he?"

But the voice over her phone was muffled. She cursed, frowning. The underground stations around Paris were notorious for spotty connection. She moved a few feet to the right, and suddenly the voice came clear again.

"He's there with you. Your signatures are right on top of each other!"

Adele lowered the phone, turning like a turret, desperately trying to take it all in. Pedestrians were now moving from the train, spilling through the doors and hastening past her and up the stairs back into the light and fresh air.

Adele, for her part, remained rigid, looking one way then the other, her heart pounding desperately. She didn't see anything... What had she expected?

She pressed her teeth tightly against each other, thinking... trying so desperately to just *think*. If he was down here, then had he just walked past her? Her eyes bounced from one pedestrian moving up the stairs to the next. But none of them were familiar. There had to be at least twenty of them... Most of them the wrong age or gender...

None of them matching the driver's license photo of Timothe Vernier.

She huffed, picking up her pace and moving further down the platform to gain a better look at the furthest doors near the back tunnel.

Her phone crackled again as she moved through more spotty reception. But try as she might, she didn't spot anything untoward.

"Can you help me here, Sami? Any movement on the phone?"

More static. She retreated back to her original position by the column. The voice came through again. "Only initially. But it's stopped again. You should be right on it, Agent Sharp."

Adele suppressed a hiss of frustration. She began to shake her head, muttering as she did. No one matched the description... no familiar faces. Where... The train flashed warnings above the doors. She had a split-second decision. Stay on the platform or board the train. She hadn't seen the killer yet... So it made sense he was still on board, didn't it?

"Sami, make sure the arriving cops stop all those pedestrians," she barked. "Don't let anyone leave the lot without being searched."

"They're thirty seconds away. Almost on you."

Adele nodded, slowly. "I can hear the sirens," she murmured.

It was a fifty-fifty shot. If she stayed and the killer was on the train still, she was going to let him escape. If he'd disembarked and she boarded, he'd also escape.

Was there a victim with him? She hadn't seen anyone. But now, glancing through the windows on the train, nothing stood out either.

The warning lights flashing above the train doors were starting to blink faster. The doors began to swish shut. Adele made a desperate decision.

She flung herself forward and stopped in the middle of the sliding doors. She didn't get on, but she didn't remain fully on the platform either.

The door started buzzing angrily. She heard a voice over the intercom asking passengers to stay clear of the doors. But while the rubber guard of the doors bounced off her chest and back, it didn't hurt. These trains were designed to avoid causing injury.

This gave her a few precious seconds longer to decide.

No suspicious activity on the platform. None on the train that she could see.

What was she missing?

Adele ignored the buzzing door. Ignored the instructions over the intercom and the odd looks cast her way from the seated commuters.

She only had moments to make a decision. She could try to stop the train, but it seemed much more likely the killer would make his escape with her distracted.

She felt a surge of frustration as the doors bounced open and tried to close again. The voice over the intercom grew terse, angrier. If anything, the warning buzz from the door was louder. She couldn't spot anything indecorous *on* the train, nor on the platform. Where *was* he?

And just then, a thought struck her.

Timothe had proven adept at avoiding cameras. Not just back at the train station where he'd broken one of the lenses but also a year ago when he'd snuck in the side door to kill Ms. Wallen.

So Adele desperately searched out the cameras in the ceiling across the platform; her eyes darted until she found a small, black eye in the sky. She spotted another. And then another. It was difficult to make out which direction the cameras were facing but her own experience in security allowed for something of an educated guess. She glanced along the platform, eyes desperately searching for…

There.

She didn't need to know where the cameras were facing. She needed to know where they *weren't*.

At the back of the train there was a section that would not have been visible when she had initially entered the underground; a small area of the platform but one that might have hidden a person.

A horrible prickling sensation spread down her spine. The voice from her phone was saying something, but she didn't hear. Couldn't.

She slipped out from between the doors. They sealed shut. The train began to scrape and squeal as it picked up pace, hastening away. The loud, reverberating rumble filled the space; most of the commuters had already left. From outside, she heard sirens… voices. Backup had arrived. She didn't know if Agent Renee was with them. But for the moment, she had to make a call.

She stood on the very edge of the platform, staring at the blind spot.

The only path killer could have taken to avoid cameras was back *onto* the tracks. There would have been just enough space behind the train for him to slip through into the tunnel.

The question now, was he alone? Or did he have a victim with him?

Adele could feel her heart beating. She knew she had to choose.

The killer clearly knew the train stations.

He seemed to like hiding in the dark; he liked avoiding direct confrontation, preferring to mock from behind the protection of his internet connection and phone service. He liked the dark, and she was now staring at the darkest portion of the station. And there... just within the mouth—was that a service door on the tracks?

"Sami!" she yelled. "Call the station. No trains can come through here. Got it?"

A crackle of a response.

"All of them!" Adele barked, already moving again. And then she slipped her phone in her pocket and broke into a sprint. She raced to the edge of the platform, peering into the dark, her heart hammering horribly, her breath caught in her throat as she fixated on the tracks, certain now that she could see the faintest outline of a service door.

The killer had been a step ahead this entire time... but she felt like she was gaining now.

In the end, it really wasn't much of a choice. She knew what she *had* to do.

Adele clambered down the edge of the concrete barrier, wincing as her side scraped against the platform. Then, teeth clenched, hands tensed against the ledge, she let go, dropping onto the tracks.

She was careful to avoid the metal rail, remembering what she'd once been told about the electrical current; she wasn't sure if this was true. But better play it safe, stepping between the rails. She hastened into the dark tunnel. The reception on the phone now died.

She could only hope Agent Sami had gotten the memo. For now, she didn't see any oncoming trains. The tracks were smooth and quiet—no rumbling, and no distant growling engine.

She hastened further into the dark, her breathing desperate. She wondered if she ought to pull out her phone and turn on the flashlight.

As she peered into the dark, to face the section of tunnel illuminated by security lights, she suddenly stiffened. There were small stone steps like a pyramid. Both sides culminated in a metal door.

The door was ajar.

No cameras, no witnesses. Adele was alone in the dark on the train tracks, staring at the hidden door.

Her heart was in her throat. She felt her skin buzz. She wasn't sure what to do. Call for help?

She knew he would be in there. He *had* to be—process of elimination told her that the killer was behind that door.

She shifted uncomfortably as she reached the bottom step, one hand reaching out and grabbing the cold rail.

Again, uncertainty came back to her. She let out a little huff of air, scratching and wincing against the throbbing pain in her side. Her exhaustion weighed heavy; her limbs felt like lead.

But she had to trust her instincts.

She let out a sigh and began taking the concrete steps. Her feet slapped against the stone, her hand trailing along the rail, feeling the strange grit of the rough surface.

And that was when she heard the scream.

An earsplitting, bloodcurdling shout, coming from inside the doorway at the top of the stairs.

She heard a voice responding, shushing, but then an even louder cry.

Her phone was dead. She was alone. Renee was nowhere to be seen; no one even knew where she was.

But another scream was all she needed to hear to break into a dead sprint, surging up the concrete steps and slamming through the open door.

She jolted into a small service space. Brass pipes and electrical boxes lined the walls. There were buttons and flashing lights and levers Adele didn't recognize.

But she *did* recognize the man standing in the middle of the room with his hands wrapped around a woman's neck.

He looked sharply over, a stunned expression on his face.

The woman in his hands was struggling something fierce. Her hair had fallen out of place, her face red, her cheeks bulging as she drew air and then let out a bellowing screech right in Timothe's face.

Adele scrambled for her weapon.

The killer cursed and tried to spin around, placing his victim between himself and the agent.

"Stand back!" Adele yelled. "Get away from her! Get back!" But she might as well have been speaking Greek. The man didn't react, didn't respond; he glared with a menacing look in his eyes.

And then he said, quietly. "I *know* you."

Adele felt a shiver creep up her spine.

CHAPTER TWENTY SEVEN

Adele stood in the small custodial space, facing the killer. She kept her gun tilted off to the side as she knew she didn't have a clean shot.

Timothe Vernier looked like the before picture in one of those glow-up ads online. The year since Ms. Wallen's death clearly hadn't treated him kindly. His hair was thinning now. His skin horribly oily and textured. His hands were pale, clammy, and his eyes kept blinking as if he had something in them. He'd gained a good thirty pounds, also, compared to his driver's license photo, but the weight had nearly exclusively gone to his cheeks and neck. The disproportionate distribution of additional poundage gave him the look as if he might topple in a breeze.

Still, his eyes fixed on her, and he repeated. "I know you... I saw you on the movie." He nodded, his cheeks wobbling. He let out a little giggle of delight as he studied Adele like a butcher might stare at a slab of meat.

She swallowed, holding back any comment at first until she'd properly assessed the situation.

At the same time, his round cheek grazed the woman's neck. His lips moved slowly, whispering something in his victim's ear, while at the same time, he pulled something out of the black bag at his feet. The two of them shuffled, struggling, one foot kicking the bag, the woman's foot trampling the straps.

But then, after another struggle, Vernier managed to withdraw the item he'd been reaching for.

A hacksaw.

Now, he gripped the woman's neck with one hand, the other brandishing his ridged blade, waving it above his head, a mad glint in his eyes.

Adele noticed something else. Despite his anger, despite the fact that he'd been interrupted in a murder attempt, his lips formed a small little simpering smile which was out in full, directed toward Adele.

The smile sent shivers up her spine.

"Go away!" he was saying toward Adele. "Get out of here, you're not wanted. You can't get between us!"

Adele kept her gun raised, but redirected. She needed a clean shot.

She sidestepped, but Timothe seemed to realize what she'd intended, and he moved just as quickly, glaring at her as he did.

Adele shot a look over her shoulder toward the open service door. She thought she heard voices from the platform now.

"We're in here!" she called out. But the sound was swallowed by the echoing of the train tunnel.

Timothe did *not* seem happy about the shout. He dug his fingers into the woman's throat, squeezing. She gasped, choking, trying to push away, but he was stronger.

"I said get out!" Vernier screamed. Just as quickly, his voice dropped, and he whispered in his victim's ear. "It's alright, sweet one. I'm going to take good care of you. I promise." He looked up again, still smiling that creepy little grin of his.

"Sir," Adele said cautiously, wetting her lips, "this doesn't end well for anyone if you don't lower that weapon and release the woman. Step back, please."

He snorted at her, but again whispered in his victim's ear. "I won't let them separate us, my dear. Not again. I promise."

"Timothe," Adele said sharply, "that isn't Ms. Wallen. It isn't her."

He looked up now, his expression flickering in confusion. "I—I know that," he snapped suddenly. Again, he was angry. But his cheeks creased as he bit back a retort, looking uncertainly at the woman in his grasp. He let out a small huff of air. "I... I know it's not..." he murmured.

"You killed her," Adele said insistently, trying to redirect his attention back toward her. "You killed your girlfriend last year. You cut off her hand."

The would-be victim's eyes widened in panic at this comment. She began to struggled fiercely, trying to bite Vernier's fingers. This only made him angrier and he dug his hands into her throat as if trying to find her spine.

She gagged, her face red, her eyes straining. Adele yelled, trying to distract him again. "Did she say something? Is that why you killed her?"

His grip loosened somewhat on the woman's throat. He stared at Adele, frowning again as if in confusion. "You knew my love? How?"

Adele shook her head. "I never met her in person. Why did you kill her?"

"She... she was stolen," he whispered. Then he shook his head again. "Idiot!" he added with a scream. He pushed his lips against the woman's cheek again. "I'll save us both. Just trust me. It'll be like that

140

time in Spain. Remember that?" He gave a playful little giggle. He used the hacksaw to slowly brush her hair from her face.

The panic in the woman's eyes was well past terror at this point. But there was nothing Adele could do without putting her in direct danger. She watched for an opening, trying to step to the side one way, then the next.

Vernier, back and forth, continued his strange mutterings. One moment, he issued threats, tried to strangle his victim, and the next, he whispered sweet nothings in her ear. The combination only further terrified the poor woman.

Adele tried to catch her eye, to communicate without speaking. She needed a clear shot. Needed the woman to duck, to move.

But the terror in the would-be victim's eyes, the desperation of the situation, had ruled out any coordination between the two of them.

"This isn't my fault!" Timothe was saying now. "I didn't do it. It wasn't me. I had to. She was the one who was going to leave *me*!" he screamed. Then he leaned in, his lips pursed, and he kissed his victim on the cheek. Just as quickly, he slipped back into his rant. "It's all the greed. These little trinkets—what are they worth? Nothing compared to true love! Show her! Show the bitch cop! Show! Do it!" One moment, he screamed, the next he leaned in, his lips grazing the woman's ear. "Please show her," he murmured.

Terrified, and clearly not understanding the directions, the victim stood frozen in place. Adele, though, pointed at the woman's wrist. "The bracelet?" she asked. "It's a very nice bracelet..." A golden, emerald-studded thing swished and swayed as the woman struggled in the killer's grasp.

Adele was doing her best to keep calm, to keep focused, but she was quickly running out of options. The killer was growing more and more agitated. She needed to do *something*. Standing by to watch a murder wasn't an option.

The killer reacted poorly to her words, however. "Nice?" he screeched. "Nice! It's a rotten, materialistic, greed-infested thing of damnation! It's her fault!"—he squeezed the woman's neck—"that I killed her! I didn't want to! Now get out of here. You're no one to stand between destiny."

"Hmm," Adele said. "Mind if we ask *her* about this destiny of yours?" Mostly, Adele was hoping the killer might release his grip on her neck. By now, she was rasping for air, her face turning blue.

But the killer seemed wise to Adele's methods and kept his grip in place. He began to raise the hacksaw, flashing his creepy smile again.

As he did, though, Adele said the first thing that came to mind. "Bernice came to me, you know. I lied earlier. I did know her. I just didn't know how to tell you."

Again, the mention of his murdered girlfriend redirected his attention. "You... you knew her?"

Adele nodded fiercely. "She said she loved you too. You know that?"

He blinked owlishly, his grip loosening somewhat. At least for the moment he wasn't choking his victim. She just needed him to step back. Needed him to step aside.

His face was cast in shadows as he swayed in and out beneath the single, naked lightbulb above. Briefly, Adele considered shooting the light. But the darkness would serve him as much as it hurt her. She wasn't the one with her hand on a woman's neck.

No... no, she decided she needed to see. But she also needed him distracted. She pressed on. "She wanted to know if you'd join her," Adele said. "She was talking to Mr. Weeks about a position in the company for you especially. She missed you. That's what she told me."

He stared at her, his voice wavering. "Liar," he whispered.

But Adele didn't blink. He was fishing. Somewhere in that fractured, strange mind of his, he thought perhaps she really was telling the truth.

"No, I'm not lying," Adele said. "She *wanted* you to take her key. The one for the side door. Remember that?"

But his expression suddenly curdled. His nostrils flared. He glared at her in fury and hissed through his teeth. "Lying whore!" he screamed. "I *took* that key! She told me never to touch it! I did that! I stole it—I knew what Weeks was doing. Little *Anton*. All she spoke about was that idiot. I saw him a few days ago, you know. He was too drunk to stand up. Ha! And she wanted to be with *him* over me!"

Adele noted this last part. Timothe had *seen* Weeks when he was knockout drunk? Had he planted that phone in his old rival's house? She wouldn't have put it past him.

But now, she'd clearly agitated the man. His voice was rising in volume, his hand tightening on his victim's neck again. He was bringing the hacksaw down.

Adele had to do *something*.

It wasn't exactly a plan. More a quick thought. But the killer was the type to taunt and belittle and mock...

Especially when he had the upper hand.

But she was now staring right at him. There was no more hiding

142

behind computer monitors or voice scramblers. No more room for pretense. He couldn't play-act. He wasn't the suave, in-control monster he'd pretended to be.

He was a wild, erratic killer whose only self-esteem was derived from harming and blaming others. There was no reasoning with such fools.

But scaring them?

Fear made even jackals scatter.

And so as he raised his saw, Adele endeavored to scare the poser. She raised her gun sharply and fired twice at the ceiling.

The sound retorted in the small room like a thunderclap. Her own ears rang. Two faint trickles of dust fell from the holes in the drywall. But the killer reacted in a panic. He froze at the first shot, then squeaked, eyes wide, and *shoved* his victim into Adele.

Initially, she felt a rush of triumph as he loosed his grip. But then the two women collided. Adele stumbled. Her gun was knocked from her hand. It went skittering off beneath one of the large, metal breaker boxes.

She cursed, trying to rise while also doing her best to avoid causing harm to the woman. The killer's would-be victim was blubbering, pleading, her hands scrambling desperately at Adele's shoulder, her face.

Adele was busy pushing to her feet. But she caught a knee to the chin for her efforts as the killer raced past her, hotfooting out of the small, custodial closet with a shout.

Adele watched him flee down the steps, cursing and massaging at her chin. Her fingers scraped beneath the breaker box, searching desperately for her weapon. But she couldn't find it. It had slid too far.

"Ma'am!" Adele yelled. "Please, are you okay?"

The woman was sobbing but nodding, makeup streaking her face. She was desperately scrambling to pull that horrible bracelet off her wrist. Tearing and twisting and trying whatever she could. Adele wanted to help, wanted to hold the woman's shaking hands and calm her down, telling her it would be okay.

But the sound of the retreating footsteps galvanized her to action.

Once she was certain the woman was fine, Adele yelled, "Shut the door! Don't let anyone back in unless they show you a police ID. Got it? I'll send help. And... and try to find my gun, if you can."

Adele winced, casting about a final time in search of her weapon.

But it was somewhere beneath the large breaker box, which by the looks of things was soldered to the wall.

There was no going after the weapon. Not while Vernier made good his getaway. Adele huffed in frustration, carefully pulled her arm from the desperate woman's grasp, and then broke into a sprint, darting through the service door and vaulting the small, metal rail onto the tracks.

Timothe was ahead of her, moving slower than she would be able to, already huffing and holding at his side as if he had a stitch.

Adele broke into a dead run, head down, arms pumping. She desperately shouted for backup. But the police were on the platform behind her.

Vernier was running in the clear opposite direction, further into the dark tunnel.

"This way!" Adele screamed back. "Suspect on foot! Send backup!"

She wasn't even sure if anyone heard her words. She thought she detected the faint buzz of radio chatter behind her, the sound of barking voices. Then footsteps.

But no time to look. Vernier was racing as fast as he could go. He'd already had a good head start, and she was losing track of him in the dark.

She was faster, but it was difficult to navigate the underground tunnel. The tracks were a threat. And every now and then, she was reminded of what she'd been told about touching the metal. She still wasn't sure if this was true or not, but it definitely hampered her progress of pursuit.

"Go away!" Vernier screamed over his shoulder. He tried to shout something else but the words died in favor of a deep, huffing puff of air.

Like this, the two of them raced forward, across the tracks. Adele didn't bother to shout after him, and he didn't bother to shout back. Small pinpricks of red and white lights blinked from the ceiling every so often, not so much illuminating anything as likely indicating where wiring or important service hatches were located.

Otherwise, the two of them moved in absolute darkness. Now, the sound of their huffing breaths, thumping footfalls echoed around them. Timothe was out of shape, but determined. She had to at least recognize this.

If she didn't catch up to him, he would slip away.

Now, they knew what he looked like. But cornered animals did desperate things. The last thing she wanted was for that man to start going postal in a crowded train station. She wasn't sure if he had other weapons on him, but he was still gripping the blue handle of his hacksaw, holding the top arc of metal. The blade swished back and forth at his side with each step, and he maintained his hold, loath to lose the thing.

Adele, for her part, was unarmed. Her gun was gone. She had never been the type to carry a backup weapon like John so often did. She'd found that ankle holsters only made her uncomfortable.

Now, though, she wished she'd held onto her weapon. Arms pumping like pistons, she moved faster and faster through the dark tunnel, her lungs aching. The stitches in her side protested with each rapid footfall. Technically, the doctor had suggested she avoid long periods of exertion.

But it wasn't like she had a choice. Wasn't like she—

She went still. Frowning.

Silence.

Why was there silence?

She blinked, waving fingers in front of her eyes.

But she could barely see a thing. They'd hit a section of the underground tunnel without a light to speak of. She couldn't even hear the voices behind them now, they'd come too far.

The silence carried the ominous implication that Vernier was no longer moving either. Briefly, she held her breath, listening.

She thought she could hear his shaking, gulping gasps for air. But the sounds echoed off the tunnel, creating a confusing amalgam of acoustics.

Adele looked one way, then the other, but she was only confronted by darkness. The huffing sound faded now too.

A faint prickle began to creep up her spine.

Ting.

Was that a footstep on metal?

Thud. Movement behind her?

She whirled around, swiping a hand through the space, but catching only air. Desperately, her fingers scrambled for her pocket in search of her phone. She needed a light. A light would help *him* locate her, but it would also do the opposite. And in a fight, she would have to trust her instincts.

She'd followed the predator into a dark corner, and now she'd have to face the consequences.

Faint tremors crept up her spine. Her fingertips prickled and buzzed. She looked one way, then the other. Every part of her wanted to turn and run. She hated the dark. She'd been recently stabbed in the dark.

And that's when she heard the faint giggling sound.

She frowned. The hairs stood on end along her arms.

The giggling sound was coming from off to her left... coming closer... closer.

No.

Not closer. Louder.

She held back a curse, her lips tight, and she finally managed to wrangle her phone from her pocket and shine the light off toward the source of the sound.

Nothing. No movement.

Where was the bastard?

But then she spotted it.

A small cellphone resting on the tracks. The giggling was coming from the phone. She stared at it. And then her eyes widened and she whirled around just as something slashed into the back of her neck.

She'd moved just in time. The hacksaw wasn't technically a hacking weapon. Nor was it particularly sharp. Still, the teeth scored a shallow cut across her neck, and Adele yelled as she tripped over one of the railroad ties. The motion, though, sent the saw clattering.

Vernier cursed, surging toward her.

But as Adele shoved roughly back to her feet, using her momentum to distance herself, the man panicked again. He broke into a sprint once more, racing in the same direction he'd been going earlier. This time, she spotlighted him with her light.

"Stop running!" she shouted. "You're only making it worse!" She dabbed at her neck, pulling away fingers stained with blood. A shallow cut, but she didn't want to think of all the bacteria and germs sitting on that blade. She also didn't want to think too much about all the horrible needles and shots and medicines she'd have to take just to make sure she wasn't infected.

The killer wasn't speaking now, though. All the air in his lungs was currently being used to manage his deep, gulping breaths.

Adele picked up the pace again, sweaty, her neck bleeding, her side throbbing horribly. She winced, peering ahead.

A light?

Was that...

Then a rumble.

The tracks began to shudder. She cursed. The trains were supposed to be grounded, but she didn't know how far they'd come. Was there another station ahead?

The train was coming fast, though, the light ahead of her illuminating the tunnel now. Perhaps a few hundred feet away. If she hugged the wall, perhaps she'd be safe. But she wasn't sure. Adele hadn't exactly studied blueprints of the layout down here in preparation.

This was all proceeding by the seat of her pants.

She had a quick choice to make.

But Vernier, she noticed, was ahead of her again, making a beeline toward something. He'd broken into a sprint with renewed vigor, as if...

And then her eyes widened as she spotted it.

A platform. He'd found a platform. He was trying to reach it before the train reached them.

Adele's only options were to pursue him and follow his lead or hug the wall and hope the train didn't hit her. The ground was shaking so horribly now that her teeth were rattling.

She cursed. She couldn't let Timothe get away.

Besides, the walls on both sides of her didn't look particularly wide. Dying by turning into goo beneath an oncoming train wasn't high on her bucket list of achievements.

So she redoubled her pace, practically screaming with the exertion as she hurtled through the dark, hastening in pursuit of Mr. Vernier.

He was gasping, desperately trying to crawl onto the platform. Huffing and wincing. He didn't seem to have the upper body strength to make it. But then she watched where he moved a few paces down. The light of the train now illuminated him. Adele cursed, flinging herself toward the ledge as well.

The train was twenty meters away.

Vernier finally found a foothold and flung himself onto the platform.

Adele followed, but received a kick to her chin. Ten meters.

The train wasn't stopping. This particular platform looked dusty, old, abandoned.

She flung herself onto the ledge again. And again received a kick to the—

But she caught it, the blow glancing off her arm. And, last minute, she rolled onto the platform, letting out a deep, whooshing gasp of air as the train breezed past. The scraping squeal of the machine against the tracks set her teeth on edge.

She lay on her back, wincing, bleeding, groaning. She wanted to take a breather.

But she didn't have the time.

Vernier was already struggling to his feet. Sleepless nights, more than one injury, and a kick to the face still hadn't deterred Adele from catching up with her target. But now, more than anything, she needed to bring him down. She couldn't let him get away.

Black spots were dancing over her eyes, suggesting she was now fading fast.

She hurtled forward, racing toward him.

But Vernier was gassed now. He let out a desperate howl and spun around, arms outstretched. He tried to shove her back onto the tracks, but Adele had been expecting it this time and twisted out of the way.

Just the two of them on this abandoned, defunct train platform. The howl and squeal of the train masking most of their heavy breathing, their desperate movements.

Wide eyes met wide eyes. Panting breaths met panting breaths.

The two of them faced each other, both as tense as could be. Vernier was trying now to maneuver, one slow step at a time, past Adele toward a set of stairs.

Adele, though, kept moving to cut him off. "Can't go that way," she muttered. "Door's closed. Just me and you down here, Timothe."

His eyes widened in panic, and he shot a look up the stairs. She could see the moment when the blood drained from his face as he spotted what she had.

Caution tape wrapped around a metal door. The sort of door that might have been pulled over the glass display of a jewelry store.

He let out a faint whimper and looked the other direction now.

"No," Adele said, between breaths, "not that way either," she murmured. "Another train might be coming... There's no other platforms for"—a pause to inhale—"miles." She wiped some sweat from her neck. Her hand pulled away bloody.

She didn't care though. Her glare was fixated on Vernier, who was now shaking like a leaf, his head shifting rapidly back and forth. She allowed her words to sink in, the acid in her tone prompting a widening of Vernier's eyes.

He took a stumbling step away, but she followed now.

"Please..." he moaned, holding up a hand as if to stave off her attack. "Please... I—I didn't mean... I didn't think..." His voice caught, and his lower lip trembled.

She just glared. He was raising a hand like the one he'd severed. Fingers splayed like the one he'd removed. She could still remember his taunting; how he'd enjoyed leading them on. But there was no phone here now. Nowhere to hide.

She was now in control, and he was pleading.

She stalked him down as he kept stumbling back along the platform, looking desperately for some sort of escape. But he was trapped, and he knew it.

"The phone," Adele said quietly, as she continued marching toward him, her shadow spreading across the floor like a harbinger. "The one in Anton Weeks's home—did you plant it?"

Without warning, the killer screamed. At the mention of Anton's name, he lunged for Adele. It was a pathetic, weak motion. His hands wrapped around her leg, and he clung on desperately. She shoved at his head hard. But he gripped her ankle, refusing to let go, like a child dragged across the floor gripping a beloved parent.

Adele thwacked him across the head. "Let go! Let go!" she demanded.

It wasn't really a fight. He posed no real threat, hugging her leg. If anything, it was more disgusting than dangerous. But proximity in such scenarios was never a good idea. He might have another weapon.

But for the moment, he hadn't procured one. She extricated herself with a quick shove of her foot and stepped back. "Hands where I can see them!" she barked.

Normally, the arresting part was done at the end of a weapon, or with backup. Now, it just felt awkward, with him still stumbling back, her moving after him. He was on his rump now, shuffling with his legs. He would soon run out of platform.

"I didn't plant anything!" he yelled at her, his hands still upraised to protect his face, then dropping again to continue to shuffle away. "It was his cleaning lady. I bribed her with an earring. A single, stupid earring! Can you believe that. She thought I was his brother, pulling a prank. It's just jewelry! Just stupid jewelry!" He was shaking now, his face red. His head trembled and his jowls wobbled. "I loved her!" he moaned. "I loved her, but she was going to leave me for Anton! She told me!"

"I don't care," Adele said firmly. "Lower your hands and turn around." She was reaching for her cuffs now.

Finally, Mr. Vernier's back bumped against the far wall. There was nowhere left for him to crawl. Nowhere left for him to hide.

He balled up, trembling, tears streaming down his face. She could see the way he tensed, cornered as he was now. Could see the decision occur to him all at once. Her back was still to the train tracks. With a sudden howl, he lunged up, shoving at her. But again, she stepped out of the way, easily enough.

He stumbled forward, nearly tripping onto the tracks, but it was Adele who caught his shirt.

She pulled him back and in the same motion cuffed his left arm, twisting it up.

"Stop moving," she said simply. Dispassionately. The metal of her cuffs was warm to the touch thanks to the friction from her sprint through the train tunnel. As she twisted Mr. Vernier's arm, she cuffed his wrists, pulling them up behind his back. As the final cuff clicked into place, Vernier slumped, all fight gone now.

She pulled him toward the metal door wrapped in caution tape. Her other hand moved toward her phone.

He was still talking, pleading his case, apologizing, begging, threatening. Just words, though.

She remembered what she'd thought about Renee earlier. She remembered why she loved him. Words were cheap. Everyone could use them. John was a man of action… and his own type of character. He wasn't perfect. She knew that much.

"Stay here!" she commanded, pushing Vernier out of the way, his back toward her, his face toward the metal door.

Her phone was now in her hand. Up the stairs of the defunct train station, though, she glimpsed a flash of blue light. Then the sound of sirens and voices. Agent Sami must have been tracking her the entire time.

She felt a flutter of relief as police suddenly poured down the steps, racing toward the sealed metal gate and shouting things like, "I see her! She has him! Look! Right there!"

Booted feet hit the stairs. Blue uniforms shifted as men and women rushed toward her.

Adele wanted to smile, but grimaced instead. The pain along her neck was still pulsing. She was pretty sure her stitches had ripped. At the very least, her bandage felt heavier now.

She looked away from Vernier, ignoring his protests, his cries.

This was what weakness looked like. And despite what Vernier kept insisting, it wasn't his girlfriend's decision to leave him that had made him into a monster.

No, it was a million little choices leading up to that moment. Some people thought character, integrity, happened in a few great moments. But in Adele's experience, those big choices were like the blooming of a plant.

The seeds were sown long ago. Choices made over a lifetime.

Choices of indulgence, of entitlement, of selfishness. And then, when life got tough, or danger came, the true nature of the person was revealed.

Vernier's nature was that of a self-obsessed narcissist.

But as she stood there, watching the police bring pliers down the stairs to tend to the lock on the sliding metal door, Adele felt a surge of guilt.

Small choices... Like ignoring John's advice? Like being too obstinate to listen to wisdom?

She was bleeding. She'd nearly died. She'd been slower than before, and it had nearly cost her life. But most of all... she'd hurt Renee. He never would admit it. John wasn't the sort to recognize feelings unless they came up and poked him in the eye. He liked burying his emotions seven feet deep. But Adele knew he'd just been trying to protect her. To look out for her.

She felt a flash of shame. She refused to look toward the killer.

She'd been an ass the way she'd treated John.

It was a strange realization to have while standing next to a man who'd murdered multiple women. It was as she processed this odd train of thought that Adele wondered if maybe she ought to have taken some of those pain meds.

The dark spots across her eyes were widening now.

"Oh," she murmured faintly. She stumbled forward, her head striking the metal cage. The padlock had snipped. It was opening now. Police were reaching for her, and for the suspect.

She fell.

Quite literally.

Unconscious.

CHAPTER TWENTY EIGHT

The time had come.... Darkness fell quickly. His adrenaline raced as he moved from one parked car to the next, his dark hat low over his face. His dark clothing hiding him in the night.

He dove over the small fence, breathing heavily, feeling the ever-accompanying pain along his body. He raced toward a side window, footsteps rapid, heart pounding. He grinned. This was always the best part. The moment when *he* knew but *they* didn't.

Soon, though, she would know as well.

He shattered the window with his elbow. A quick blow. The sound was softened by the padding he'd stitched into his sleeve. A few of the shards of glass tapped against the floor in the basement. But he'd already scoped the place out. She slept on the other side of the house. They both did.

She also slept with a fan running. The perfect camouflage for sound.

The thrill-seeker had always prided himself on his ability to gather information and execute. Hell, it was why they'd hired him to begin with. Why Captain Renee had wanted him on the team.

Before shit had gone sideways.

He winced now, feeling the scars stretch across his back... He let out a faint, huffing sigh, dusting a few more strands of glass out toward himself where they landed silently on the grass.

No sounds behind him. No shouts. The only vector of observation would have been the second-floor window of the neighbor across the street. But the drapes were closed. Minimal risk.

This was the best point of entry.

Even as he considered his options, he was aware of just how his mind compartmentalized. He'd come to *enjoy* what he was about to do. But leading up to that moment, it was all tactical, strategic. The glass was cleared. Now he moved through the window, stepping off the heater unit against the house and using it to propel into the home.

He landed in a crouch, little more than a shadow folded in a shadow. His eyes took in the hall ahead. This, now, was unknown terrain. Recognizance could only go so far.

Inevitably, improvisation was needed.

As he crouched in the hall, taking in his surroundings and counting the doors, he clenched his teeth against a sudden spasm in his back.

Renee had left him to die.

The locals, though, when they'd found him, had decided to have some fun. They'd tried to take him apart, an inch of flesh and sinew at a time. They'd had their fun for years, leaving him in a dungeon to rot. It had taken every ounce of strength and know-how for him to escape that hellhole, cross the border and return home.

He didn't blame the insurgents for what they'd done to him.

How could he blame dead men?

He blamed Renee—and he was determined to see the captain suffer before he spent some time with John, showing him some of the tricks he'd picked up in the sweltering heat of a torturer's favorite chamber.

Renee was in for an object lesson in agony.

But first things first.

He pulled his weapon from his hip, double-checking. And then he began to move, hastening down the hall. Five minutes he'd given himself. And this time, he refused to be caught unawares.

Adele Sharp was an agent. She'd had a weapon.

But this target?

Harmless as they came.

He smirked, moving faster, feeling the pain subside as the adrenaline took over once more. The drugs rarely helped, but this sort of thing? He could get used to this… In fact, once he was finished with John, there were so many other possibilities available.

He grinned widely as he moved rapidly.

And that's when the door opened.

A faint moan of a hinges. A creak of wood. And then a child appeared in the doorway.

He froze. The child stared.

She looked like her father. Looked just like Renee. But why the hell was she in the middle room? He'd spotted the girl's bed through the window before. He wasn't here for the girl, though.

He was here for the mother. Another one of John's lovers.

Now, though, he was in something of a pickle. He tilted his head, staring at the child. Her eyes were wide, and she breathed in shallow puffs. He held a finger slowly to his lips.

It wasn't like he cared if the child lived. He'd intended to take out *everyone* Renee loved. He'd just been hoping to do it one at a time.

Perhaps the girl was a volunteer?

He'd read vaguely, somewhere, that another killer had once tried to

153

take this little girl. Perhaps that was why she reacted the way she did.

Instead of screaming, instead of freezing. She stiffened briefly, but then moved.

She didn't try to run though. No, she flung something at him. Something she'd been holding in her hand. He raised an arm instinctively. But then a small pouch burst on his skin. Dust got in his eyes.

And instantly, pain followed.

He tried to fire, but the sound of small feet scampering for safety alerted him that he'd missed. He couldn't see... He growled, blinking horribly, tears streaming, snot forming. The pain was immense. He recognized what it was, of course. Pepper balls. Powdered pepper spray.

He should've expected safety precautions. Especially from Renee's daughter. He didn't doubt that John, through his contacts, was the one who'd gotten his hand on this stuff.

And now, by proxy, Renee was putting him through another bout of sheer agony.

He almost dropped his weapon. How embarrassing would that have been? He suffered in silence, though. The silencer on his pistol had muted the two gunshots. The sound of the girl's retreating footsteps had faded. Either she was hiding, or the ringing in his ears from the pain was obscuring any noise she made.

He wiped desperately at his face. Where was the damn bathroom? Where?

He couldn't remember the layout. The pain was too intense. He remembered similar sensations back in his hellhole. Remembered how often he'd pleaded for them to just end it. He held back a shriek, held back any sounds.

He was accustomed to pain. He was determined to see this job through. He wouldn't fail again. He refused.

With thumping footsteps, far louder than he might have liked, he stumbled down the hall, blinking tears, unable to see, wiping at his face. He moved in the direction of the mother's bedroom.

Moved with his gun gripped tightly in one hand. He was going to see this through.

One way or another, he was going to take something from John that could never be given back.

It didn't matter if his eyes stung.

If he had to, he'd murder her blind.

CHAPTER TWENTY NINE

Adele blinked in the sunlight as she stepped through the sliding doors at the hospital. The small bottle of pills rattled in the white paper bag she had at her side. She was still determined not to take them. Now, though, wincing, she moved slowly, a hand occasionally darting to check on the bandage beneath her shirt.

Most of the stitches had survived the altercation with Vernier. But some had ripped. The doctor had been none too pleased.

Which was nothing compared to what Adele had felt when he'd threatened to revoke his permission for duty unless she took better care of herself.

The look on Agent Renee's face didn't help her sour mood.

John reclined on a bench outside the hospital doors, watching her. "Hi there, American Princess," he said.

"Not in the mood, John."

He beamed. "Good thing I have mood enough for two." He patted the seat next to him.

She approached but didn't sit down. It was nice to have treatment in the same hospital as the woman she'd rescued. Adele had even taken a moment to visit. "She's going to recover," she said as she approached Renee. "Full recovery. They're even letting her keep the bracelet. She said it's hers, but Vernier said she was lying. Guess they're not going with the word of a murderer."

"Good to hear," John said. "Vernier admitted to everything, by the way. Got the call an hour ago. He said it was your fault he tried to kill everyone. But... I think he thought you were his girlfriend." John's brow furrowed in confusion.

She snorted. "He was blaming everyone."

"What did the doctor say?" Renee asked in the tone of someone who'd already guessed.

"Not much. He wasn't happy. Say, why are you so chipper?" Adele muttered.

"Because Foucault says you have to rest another week."

"Says? What, like no cases?"

John nodded, beaming. "Rest. Sleep. Recover. You nearly killed yourself, Adele," he added and his smile slipped.

She sighed, running a hand through her hair.

Technically, John wasn't wrong. But there was a drastic difference between a few stitches and being flattened by a train. The second one hadn't been her fault.

"You've made your point," Adele said in a gentle tone. "Can we go now? I promise to be a good girl and not chase any more bad guys through underground tunnels."

John snorted. "Nice promise." He pushed to his feet, extending a large arm, which she took, looping hers through it.

Arm in arm, the two of them moved slowly back toward the multi-level parking structure. Adele liked the way it felt, his arm in hers. She looked up at her partner and flashed a smile. He looked back at her, but he didn't share her expression.

In fact, John was frowning.

"What's wrong?" she said.

He shook his head, his brow still furrowed. "I don't want to drive you back to your place," he said quietly.

She stared at him.

"It isn't safe, Adele. We both know it isn't…" They passed around a white security barrier, walking toward where John had parked over two handicapped spots. At least some things never changed.

"I get it," Adele murmured, as she approached the vehicle. John paused, staring at her over the roof of the car. "I really do," she said. "But that apartment is my home. I'll be fine."

John shook his head. "Foucault won't give you a bodyguard forever," he insisted. "What *then*?"

Adele shrugged. "We'll cross the bridge when—"

"We've already come to it. I'm telling you, Adele," John said, his voice firm all of a sudden. "I don't want you living there."

She glared back at him, resting her small paper bag of painkillers on the top of the sedan. "Is that a threat?"

"It's an offer," he replied. He shifted uncomfortably now, clicking the locks a couple of times, though he'd already opened them. The headlights flashed, the locks beeped. But John looked scared now. More scared than she'd ever seen him before.

"What is it?" she said. "John… John, are you alright?"

He gave a shaking little sigh. "I… I've been thinking. Long and hard."

"Good for you," she said. "I know it doesn't come naturally." She flashed a grin to show she was joking.

But rather than rising to the bait and cutting back with repartee of

156

his own, John just said, "I... I think..."

He looked at her, his eyes flashing. Then the words came out all at once, jumbled. "I want you to move in with me." He nodded firmly the moment he'd finished, crossing his arms in defiance as if daring her to tease him over this.

But the last thing on her mind was teasing John. Adele just stared. "I... *move* in? What? Like... like to live?"

"No, Adele, I'm asking you to bust a move and get jiggy with it. Yes! Like to live. I have a house."

"Yes, you do."

"You've seen it."

"I have seen your house, John."

"Well," he said, waving his hands.

She sighed. "It's a bit more complicated than knowing you have a house. And *seeing* it. There's more involved."

He snorted, slamming a hand against the roof of the car. "What more?" he demanded. "You're not safe at your place... And I... I..." He muttered something beneath his breath.

"What was that?" Adele asked, leaning in.

He muttered it again, but the handsome Frenchman's cheeks were now turning red.

Adele beamed, enjoying the moment immensely, despite the sudden sense of unease in her stomach.

John sighed, and then, loud enough for her to hear, but no one else who might have been eavesdropping, he said, "I care about you."

Adele pointed at him. "Ha!" she exclaimed. "I knew it!"

He glared. "I've said it before, dammit."

"You love me!" Adele replied. She winced, lowering her arm just as quickly. "You want to kiss me. John Renee loves me."

He glared at her and stomped around the car. He leaned in now, his tall frame twice as wide as hers. His eyes peered down, meeting hers, flashing with something just on the other side of anger. "So what if I do, Agent Sharp?"

Her smile softened. Her eyes held his. She nodded once. "I care for you too, John. I really do. I'm not trying to hurt you. I just... just..." She let out a frustrated sigh.

It stopped, though, as he leaned in, his breath warm against her cheek. He didn't quite kiss her, rather, his lips hovered near hers, brushing past her nose, along her upper lip. Then he said, "What do you say? Will you?"

She swallowed, her throat dry all of a sudden. Another reason she

157

liked being with John: things never got too familiar to become stale. He was often unpredictable in such things. And while this caused headaches, it also came with perks.

"I," she murmured, "I want to. I just... I need to think about it."

He pulled away without kissing her. He nodded once. "Fine," he said. "Think. But as long as you stay at that apartment, you're putting yourself in danger. I'll tell you what," he added. "If you stay there, you ain't gettin' none of this." He wiggled his eyebrows.

"Are you threatening a sex strike?" she asked.

John snorted. "Don't test me, Sharp. I'm a desperate man." He looked away now, moving back around the car and running a hand through his hair.

Adele watched him move, her emotions at odds. She knew she wanted to make John happy. Wanted him to feel that she was safe. But she also didn't want to give up her mother's apartment.

Her apartment.

It was all she really had left of Elise Romei. All she really had left of her past in Paris.

It was true that she'd been attacked at that place, though. True, also, that John had more than enough space.

She hesitated, slipping into the passenger seat next to John. As they buckled, she said, "So what... what are we thinking exactly? Same room? Separate rooms?"

"I sleep on the couch," John said.

"Of course you do."

"I mean... I can move it into the same room if you want."

"John, you snore. I don't know how to tell you that nicely."

John grinned. He looked at her. "You snore too. It was the biggest consideration before I made the offer."

She stared at him, scandalized, as he began to reverse out of the parking spot. "I do *not* snore," she said.

"Like a hog. Like a chainsaw through a log."

"That doesn't even make sense."

"Sure it does," John said. "I'll record you next time. I'll prove it."

She crossed her arms angrily. "I do *not* snore."

"So... does that mean you're considering it?"

She shot him a look. "Do I snore?"

He blinked. "Ah... hand to God, never heard a peep from you while sleeping. You're as quiet as wind through a bunny rabbit's fur."

"There we go," she said with a laugh.

As they backed out of the parking lot, jarring over a speed bump, the small bag of painkillers she'd accidentally left on the roof tumbled off and hit the ground. She winced, but didn't protest. She hadn't been expecting to take them anyway.

Those things muddled her thoughts. And she needed to think clearly if she was going to make a reasonable decision.

It wouldn't be so bad, moving out of her place to go live with John, would it? They'd spent nights in hotels before. But it wasn't the same thing. Not really. Life was stressful enough… She still had that interview with Foucault about the shooting. With the case solved, he'd be expecting an appointment any day.

She sighed as Renee began navigating up the street, moving away from the hospital and back in the direction of her apartment.

Hers. That was it. It was her apartment.

Interviews with Foucault aside, she didn't know if she could give that up. Not even for John.

***

She didn't mind having John around the place. And he didn't seem as if he wanted her to be on her own for even a second. She was doing her best to take this in her stride.

Now, though, curled up on the couch next to each other, she was deeply regretting her choice to let John pick the movie for the night.

"Is that…" She stared at the screen. "Is that a booger?"

"Hush," Renee whispered back. "It's an alien."

"It looks like a booger."

"It's not a booger, Adele. It's going to eat that man's face. Ha! See!"

"I see a booger giving an astronaut a hug."

John shushed her again, leaning forward in excitement as he stared at the television. At least the popcorn bowl between them wasn't stale or reheated this time. The faint scent of salty butter lingered on the air inside her apartment.

Adele was trying her best to watch the movie. The horrible, awful, never again in a million years movie.

But she was distracted. In this case, it was something of a mercy.

As she looked around, studying her home, she felt a lump in her throat. She shifted next to Renee, the warmth of his body sweaty against her knee. She shifted, creating a bit of distance between the two of them. Her eyes moved from the large floor-to-ceiling window. She could remember, nearly two decades ago, when she'd first laid eyes on it.

Her mother had rented this place. It had been Adele's second home away from Germany…

Until everything changed.

She remembered how Elise and Adele had so often sat on a similar couch, though far cheaper and lumpier at the time. The two of them had stared out the large window, watching Paris go about its day. Oftentimes, they would pick out boats on the river, making a competition of guessing which boat passed under a bridge first.

The kitchen had been nearly identical too, minus the microwave. She wondered if her mother would have been proud.

Adele felt a lump in her throat, but no matter how much she swallowed, it didn't go away.

She shifted uncomfortably, exhaling faintly.

Could she really give this all up?

Tears formed in her eyes. More memories played across her mind. She thought of story times, game nights. Laughter. Anger. Arguments. And everything in between. John's arm slipped over her shoulder, absentmindedly. As if he hadn't even noticed her pull away.

He gave a little hug, pulling her back the couple of inches. Her knee was still sweaty. She still wanted some space…

Was that such a bad thing?

She closed her eyes, wondering what Robert would say. But of course, she couldn't ask him either. She missed thinking of the world in terms of adults and children. Missed being able to go find someone for advice. For wisdom.

But now… she was the adult.

John was.

God help them.

There were no secret recipes for a successful life. No hidden words to mutter in incantation to avoid suffering and cling to happiness. In fact, in Adele's experience, happiness was a byproduct. Not a goal.

This wasn't the first time a man had asked her to move in. Robert Henry, her old mentor, had let her live at his place more than once. A home away from home away from home…

She'd had *many* places to call her home. None of them had really felt like it. Especially after her mother's passing.

That was in the past, now, though. She couldn't live there. Couldn't linger.

She swallowed again, pretending she'd gotten a piece of popcorn stuck and taking a quick sip from the glass of water on the small table at her side.

John shouted at the TV screen. "Run! Run! Haha, idiot! He's going to eat you too!"

She held back a snort of laughter. Tears in her eyes, laughter on her lips... And everything in between.

Was this what she wanted?

She remembered when she'd first left Paris to move to California. Remembered how Robert Henry had emailed her. He'd missed her. If she could do it over again, she never would have left. She knew that now.

It had meant so much to her to have a place, a person like Robert. A father figure who actually *liked* her. If she'd stayed in Paris, she could've lived with Robert in that mansion of his for years. She thought of all the memories, the time spent together.

She smiled faintly.

She couldn't hold onto the past. Not forever. She'd put pieces of that history into the grave. Other pieces she would keep as close as possible. Memories would stay, but even these could drift.

John looked so happy, slapping his knee and taunting make believe characters in a B-rated horror movie that she'd never heard of. And there she sat next to him, not sure whether to laugh or cry.

Another memory made in this apartment.

But this type could also be found elsewhere.

She sighed, a long, breathy exhalation.

She'd already made up her mind. And she knew it now.

She lowered her head, resting it against Renee's shoulder.

"John," she whispered.

"Hmm?" he said, distracted.

"In exchange for changing the movie, I'll move out."

"Mhmm."

"John, did you hear me?"

"Yeah, yeah, good one."

"John."

"What?" He looked at her suddenly, pausing the movie. "Yeah?"

"I said," she replied quietly, "I think you're right. I'd... I'd like to move in."

He stared and nearly dropped the remote. He turned on the couch, looking away from the screen now to gape at her. "Really?" he said.

She smiled at his reaction. "Really. When can I?"

"Tonight!"

"I... Well. That's cutting it close."

"Fine! Tomorrow morning!"

161

Adele tried to laugh it off. But Renee was dead serious.

"Why not?" he said. "It's not like I'm going to charge you rent."

"I—well, no. But I'd help, of course."

"Psh. Forget it. I own my house. I can get some guys to come down tomorrow and pack things. They have a truck and everything."

"Movers?"

"Oh… I mean, yeah," he said grudgingly. "I guess we could call movers instead."

"So… tomorrow morning, you're serious?"

"Why not. You barely own anything, Adele. The only place more spartan than this was Greece like a bazillion years ago." John was beaming now and pointing. "It was the movie, wasn't it? I knew you'd pick up on the theme."

"The what?"

"The aliens!"

"The boogers?"

"Yeah—they keep moving around because no galaxy is safe," John said excitedly. "It's kinda like this situation…"

Adele looked doubtfully at the screen. "You… you feel like I'm a booger being attacked by cat people."

"They're not cats, Adele," John said with a sniff. "They're sphinx-kind." He nodded primly. "The movie did it. I knew it would work. It changed your mind! It's one of my all-time favorites, you know."

"Mhmm," Adele said, deciding she didn't need to correct him in that moment. She didn't have the heart. "The movie," she said. "It convinced me."

"Ha!" John declared, pumping a fist. He leaned in suddenly, hugging her and kissing her cheek. "Tomorrow morning then! I'll make some calls right now." He pushed off the couch and gave a little jig, shimmying his hips, before hurrying toward where he'd left his phone by the door.

Adele watched, amused.

John Renee wasn't much a man of words. The ones he used were often the type that daytime television chose to censor. He didn't say "I love you" as often as some did.

But *this*, the way he was excitedly moving about, grabbing his phone, already setting things in motion to help her move… this was how he acted "I love you."

She smiled as John bobbed his head in time with the rhythm of the movie's theme song.

162

EPILOGUE

Adele shouldn't have been so surprised, she decided, when—true to his word—Agent Renee showed up in the morning with three beefy man who didn't say a word. Their muscles rippled, boasting military tattoos as, one at a time, they removed the sparse items of furniture from her home.

Adele had insisted on tending to her bedroom herself.

It wasn't like she *had* much. All of her clothing was able to fit into a single suitcase. In fact, half of her shirts were still *in* a suitcase she'd brought with her from California. Over the last couple of years in Paris, she'd never gotten around to unloading the thing.

And now, she felt a strange tiredness as she zipped it up again.

She hated moving. She'd done it her entire life. But now she wasn't moving *away* so much as moving *toward*.

That had to make a difference. John was driving the loading truck himself, barking orders like a drill instructor as his movers carried Adele's furniture. One of the men, who must have had grizzly bear in his genetics, carried the mini fridge on his own down the stairs.

Adele had already packed the items in the bathroom. She'd never much realized how few things she actually owned.

It took time to build a nest... And that was the one thing she'd never much been given in the same place.

The last person she'd lived with had been her ex-boyfriend, Angus. She'd thought he was going to propose. In the end, he'd dumped her. The Painter had then hunted him down.

Adele hefted a suitcase in one hand, two plastic bags full of toiletries in the other. She let out a faint puff of air, trying not to lean too heavily on her injured side. Things would go better this time.

At least a girl could hope.

"Adele!" John's voice echoed through the apartment. "Do you want the fridge or can we leave it?"

Adele sighed, pushing out of her bedroom suitcase first.

***

The mailman liked this route through Southern Paris. The small,

163

single-family homes often came with well-manicured lawns and hedges. One of his favorite homes to stop by was Bernadette's. He'd known her from school. And that cute kid of hers often waved when he walked by.

He smiled in anticipation, taking the steps up the front porch.

He paused suddenly, frowning.

A streak of red stained the side of the door frame. The door was open. No sign of little Claudia. No sign of Bernadette.

"Hello?" he called out tentatively, his voice shaking. "Hello, is anyone in there?"

He'd been sorting the letters, but now lowered them, holding a few like a deck of cards. He took a tentative step toward the door. Something about the red streak made his skin prickle.

Was that...

Was...

He didn't dare think it.

But what if it was?

He leaned in, staring. Paint—surely...

Paint didn't usually have a long strand of brown hair stuck to it, though.

Blood...

And as he leaned in, he spotted more blood, pooling just within the door, blocked from spilling onto the porch by the small privacy ledge. His heart pounding, he pushed the door open. It groaned, slowly creaking on hinges.

And that's when he saw the body.

One hand reaching toward the door, as if in desperation. Fingers curled, taut in rigor mortis. The woman's hair splayed out around her, like seaweed drifting on a current. His heart pounded horribly. He held back a shout. His hand was already fumbling for his phone. He dropped the letters and they spun, spun, spun, like twirling leaves. Each of those perfect, lily-white canvases now stained in red where they hit the ground.

"Bernadette?" he whispered softly. "Can you hear me?"

But she wasn't moving. He felt a prickle of horror spreading up his spine.

Faintly, he heard the sound of crying. Soft, muted murmurs coming from behind the couch. He turned sharply, gasping for air. He couldn't think. Couldn't breathe. He accidentally stepped in the blood and yelped, jerking his foot back and stumbling. Letters spilled from his open, blue bag.

But he barely noticed. His attention was caught by the faint sobbing still. "Cl-Claudia?" he whispered. "It's me. Eric. The mailman. H-hello?"

Images of boogeymen luring him to his death flashed through his mind.

The sobbing intensified. And then...

A small, tear-streaked face appeared over the back of the couch. Dark eyes blinked out. A tiny, cherubic nose sniffed a couple of times. A girl in pajamas stared at him, trembling horribly.

Eric hurried forward, doing his best to block the view of the woman on the ground. His old childhood friend. It didn't seem right leaving her there. But he'd watched enough TV to know he shouldn't disturb a crime scene...

For that's what this obviously was, wasn't it?

Shit. he thought as he spotted a footstep of blood behind him. He was going to have hell to pay... His heart skipped. What if... what if they thought *he* did it?

But Claudia was crying. He pushed aside the selfish thoughts and hastened toward the couch, holding out a hand. "Dear, it's okay. You're safe now. I promise!" He swallowed despite his words, feeling more chills along his neck. "Come out from behind there, dear. It's okay. It's going to be okay."

But Claudia refused to move. She ducked behind the couch again, quiet, still trembling.

The mailman felt a rush of grief as he remembered what that poor little girl had endured only the month before.

And now this...

Some people had all the bad luck.

His phone was connecting now. He swallowed, his voice shaking still. "H-hello?" he said when the ringtone stopped. "Hello... She—she's not moving. She looks cold... I... I think... I'd like to report a murder. Please send help."

***

John gave Adele a little hug from behind, wrapping his large arms over her shoulders. The truck tires squealed behind them as one of John's buddies had agreed to return the vehicle. The two of them now stood outside John's small, single-story, blue-painted home. She had to hand it to him—he'd prettied up the place.

The door was open, and she detected a faint scent like fabric freshener.

She paused. "Did—is that a candle?" she said.

"I wish. No. I didn't find any in time. It's detergent in a saucepan... I mean, it's basically a candle-warmer."

"Detergent in a saucepan... How sweet." Adele chuckled and gave her boyfriend's arm a quick squeeze.

John rocked on his heels, ushering her gently toward the door. He didn't push, though, didn't shove. It was more of an invitation.

One she took.

It felt strange stepping across the threshold into her new place... a shared place. At least for now...

She frowned at this thought, trying to push it from her mind. She didn't want to live in fear of the other shoe falling. Her father and mother had lived together for nearly ten years...

Until they'd divorced.

Adele bit her lip. Just within the door, she spotted her possessions stacked neatly against one wall where the movers had placed them.

"Wow," John said hesitantly. "That... that's kinda cramped, isn't it?"

She tensed. "I—I mean. You said it was okay for me to bring the table. It's okay, right?"

"Yeah... yeah, I guess..." John's voice was tinged with... *something* she couldn't quite place.

Gently, she turned in his arms, facing him now. She studied Renee's expression. "You're not getting cold feet, are you?" she asked firmly. "John, if you're getting cold feet you have to tell me. It's in the rules."

"Nothing cold about my feet," John said. "You can check if you'd like. Foot massage every Monday. That's also in the rules."

Adele snorted. "You wish."

But even as they teased, she sensed the air of unease. It hadn't occurred to her until that moment just how big of a deal this was for *him*. She'd spent so much time thinking about herself, she hadn't even considered John.

She felt a flash of guilt. Softly, she said, "We can move the table... I don't really like it anyway."

"Really?"

"No," she said. "It's old. Nasty. Yours is much better."

John beamed, giving her a quick peck on the forehead before releasing her and stepping further into the house. He aimed at various furniture and appliances, starting to rattle off what sounded like a prepared spiel. "Gotta wiggle the toaster handle for it to work... And

166

that room is yours if you want it. I really do sleep on the couch. But if you want me to cuddle…" He wiggled his eyebrows.

Adele snorted. "Right. *Cuddle*," she said with air quotes.

He grinned, a hand against the back of his head. He turned, pointing. "That's the bathroom."

"I've been here before, John."

"I know. I know. Just in case you forgot. And also, guess what!" He turned to her, grinning even more widely.

"What?"

"That movie last night? It has a sequel. I was able to find it online. We can watch the whole thing tonight *with* extended features."

Adele felt her stomach sink. She tried to pass it off as a faint smile and a nervous laugh. "Aha… Yay. That's… that's something."

John flashed a thumbs-up.

And just then, his phone began to ring.

Still smiling, he reached into his pocket and pulled the device. "Hello," Renee said, chipper. His eyes were sparkling.

Adele watched, her own frown forming as John's smile faded.

"When?" he said. "You're sure… What—*who*?"

His voice cracked like a whip all of a sudden. His smile vanished like mist beneath direct sunlight. Something in his tone scared her.

"John?" Adele said quickly. "John, what is it?"

But it was as if he were staring straight through her. The blood was leaving his cheeks. Pale, stunned, his voice shaking, Agent Renee snapped, "Where is she? Damn it, I'll snap your neck—tell me where the hell she is. And her mother?" John blinked, swallowed. And then the phone nearly fell from his hand as if his fingers had suddenly stopped working.

Quickly, he caught the device. It took him a second to place it back to his ear. He turned away from Adele now, as if shielding himself.

"Keep her there," he murmured. "How?"

Another pause.

"You're sure? Stabbed?"

Adele was now moving toward him, her own fingers fluttering to her ribs. "Renee!" she called. "Please, what's the matter?"

John lowered his phone. He turned to look at her, his hands dangling uselessly at his sides like lead weights. "She's dead," he whispered, his voice strained.

Adele felt as if she'd been slapped. Her skin prickled. "Claudia?" she said, scarcely daring to voice the name.

"W—what? No. No, thank God. She's alive. Her mother.

167

Bernadette. Someone broke into her home last night. Shot her, then stabbed her."

"*Stabbed* her?" Adele's fingers were trembling. Grief shot through her, but also horror.

He nodded, staring at Adele as if seeing her for the first time. "Oh Christ," he said. "Just like someone stabbed you... Adele... Shit— Bernadette's dead... Claudia... CHRIST!" He flung his phone across the room and it shattered against the fridge. John looked like he was trying desperately to calm down, but another surge of anger saw him punch the wall with another bellow.

His fist went straight through.

He stood there, fist buried in the wall, shoulders shaking horribly.

Adele just stood helplessly, watching Renee and feeling a cold, icy sensation form in her stomach. Perhaps moving into Renee's place hadn't been the safest option after all.

Someone had stabbed her. Then killed John's ex.

The killer wasn't after Adele.

Far, far worse... He was coming for John.

NOW AVAILABLE!

LEFT TO RUIN
(An Adele Sharp Mystery—Book 16)

The #1 bestselling series! A new serial killer strikes, and FBI Special Agent Adele Sharp can't shake the feeling that he is masquerading as normal, and right before her eyes. In a mad race against time, Adele must ask herself: who is she overlooking? And how does he blend in?

"A masterpiece of thriller and mystery."
—Books and Movie Reviews, Roberto Mattos (re Once Gone)

LEFT TO RUIN is book #16 in the #1 bestselling FBI thriller series featuring Adele Sharp (the series begins with LEFT TO DIE, book #1) by USA Today bestselling author Blake Pierce, whose #1 bestseller Once Gone (a free download) has received over 1,000 five-star reviews.

FBI Special Agent Adele Sharp—a German-and-French raised American with triple citizenship—is made to criss-cross America and Europe to bring criminals to justice. But this case is truly testing her, and as more bodies begin to appear, Adele is forced to consider: is everything really as it seems?

Or could this killer be hiding in plain sight?

A page-turning and harrowing crime thriller featuring a brilliant and tortured FBI agent, the ADELE SHARP series is a riveting mystery, packed with non-stop action, suspense, twists and turns, revelations, and driven by a breakneck pace that will keep you flipping pages late into the night. Fans of Rachel Caine, Teresa Driscoll and Robert Dugoni are sure to fall in love.

"An edge of your seat thriller in a new series that keeps you turning pages! ...So many twists, turns and red herrings... I can't wait to see what happens next."
—Reader review (Her Last Wish)

"A strong, complex story about two FBI agents trying to stop a serial killer. If you want an author to capture your attention and have you guessing, yet trying to put the pieces together, Pierce is your author!"
—Reader review (Her Last Wish)

"A typical Blake Pierce twisting, turning, roller coaster ride suspense thriller. Will have you turning the pages to the last sentence of the last chapter!!!"
—Reader review (City of Prey)

"Right from the start we have an unusual protagonist that I haven't seen done in this genre before. The action is nonstop... A very atmospheric novel that will keep you turning pages well into the wee hours."
—Reader review (City of Prey)

"Everything that I look for in a book... a great plot, interesting characters, and grabs your interest right away. The book moves along at a breakneck pace and stays that way until the end. Now on go I to book two!"
—Reader review (Girl, Alone)

"Exciting, heart pounding, edge of your seat book... a must read for mystery and suspense readers!"
—Reader review (Girl, Alone)

Blake Pierce

Blake Pierce is the USA Today bestselling author of the RILEY PAGE mystery series, which includes seventeen books. Blake Pierce is also the author of the MACKENZIE WHITE mystery series, comprising fourteen books; of the AVERY BLACK mystery series, comprising six books; of the KERI LOCKE mystery series, comprising five books; of the MAKING OF RILEY PAIGE mystery series, comprising six books; of the KATE WISE mystery series, comprising seven books; of the CHLOE FINE psychological suspense mystery, comprising six books; of the JESSE HUNT psychological suspense thriller series, comprising twenty four books; of the AU PAIR psychological suspense thriller series, comprising three books; of the ZOE PRIME mystery series, comprising six books; of the ADELE SHARP mystery series, comprising sixteen books, of the EUROPEAN VOYAGE cozy mystery series, comprising four books; of the new LAURA FROST FBI suspense thriller, comprising nine books (and counting); of the new ELLA DARK FBI suspense thriller, comprising eleven books (and counting); of the A YEAR IN EUROPE cozy mystery series, comprising nine books, of the AVA GOLD mystery series, comprising six books (and counting); of the RACHEL GIFT mystery series, comprising eight books (and counting); of the VALERIE LAW mystery series, comprising nine books (and counting); of the PAIGE KING mystery series, comprising six books (and counting); of the MAY MOORE mystery series, comprising six books (and counting); and the CORA SHIELDS mystery series, comprising three books (and counting).

An avid reader and lifelong fan of the mystery and thriller genres, Blake loves to hear from you, so please feel free to visit www.blakepierceauthor.com to learn more and stay in touch.

BOOKS BY BLAKE PIERCE

CORA SHIELDS MYSTERY SERIES
UNDONE (Book #1)
UNWANTED (Book #2)
UNHINGED (Book #3)

MAY MOORE SUSPENSE THRILLER
NEVER RUN (Book #1)
NEVER TELL (Book #2)
NEVER LIVE (Book #3)
NEVER HIDE (Book #4)
NEVER FORGIVE (Book #5)
NEVER AGAIN (Book #6)

PAIGE KING MYSTERY SERIES
THE GIRL HE PINED (Book #1)
THE GIRL HE CHOSE (Book #2)
THE GIRL HE TOOK (Book #3)
THE GIRL HE WISHED (Book #4)
THE GIRL HE CROWNED (Book #5)
THE GIRL HE WATCHED (Book #6)

VALERIE LAW MYSTERY SERIES
NO MERCY (Book #1)
NO PITY (Book #2)
NO FEAR (Book #3)
NO SLEEP (Book #4)
NO QUARTER (Book #5)
NO CHANCE (Book #6)
NO REFUGE (Book #7)
NO GRACE (Book #8)
NO ESCAPE (Book #9)

RACHEL GIFT MYSTERY SERIES
HER LAST WISH (Book #1)
HER LAST CHANCE (Book #2)

HER LAST HOPE (Book #3)
HER LAST FEAR (Book #4)
HER LAST CHOICE (Book #5)
HER LAST BREATH (Book #6)
HER LAST MISTAKE (Book #7)
HER LAST DESIRE (Book #8)

AVA GOLD MYSTERY SERIES
CITY OF PREY (Book #1)
CITY OF FEAR (Book #2)
CITY OF BONES (Book #3)
CITY OF GHOSTS (Book #4)
CITY OF DEATH (Book #5)
CITY OF VICE (Book #6)

A YEAR IN EUROPE
A MURDER IN PARIS (Book #1)
DEATH IN FLORENCE (Book #2)
VENGEANCE IN VIENNA (Book #3)
A FATALITY IN SPAIN (Book #4)

ELLA DARK FBI SUSPENSE THRILLER
GIRL, ALONE (Book #1)
GIRL, TAKEN (Book #2)
GIRL, HUNTED (Book #3)
GIRL, SILENCED (Book #4)
GIRL, VANISHED (Book 5)
GIRL ERASED (Book #6)
GIRL, FORSAKEN (Book #7)
GIRL, TRAPPED (Book #8)
GIRL, EXPENDABLE (Book #9)
GIRL, ESCAPED (Book #10)
GIRL, HIS (Book #11)

LAURA FROST FBI SUSPENSE THRILLER
ALREADY GONE (Book #1)
ALREADY SEEN (Book #2)
ALREADY TRAPPED (Book #3)
ALREADY MISSING (Book #4)
ALREADY DEAD (Book #5)

ALREADY TAKEN (Book #6)
ALREADY CHOSEN (Book #7)
ALREADY LOST (Book #8)
ALREADY HIS (Book #9)

EUROPEAN VOYAGE COZY MYSTERY SERIES
MURDER (AND BAKLAVA) (Book #1)
DEATH (AND APPLE STRUDEL) (Book #2)
CRIME (AND LAGER) (Book #3)
MISFORTUNE (AND GOUDA) (Book #4)
CALAMITY (AND A DANISH) (Book #5)
MAYHEM (AND HERRING) (Book #6)

ADELE SHARP MYSTERY SERIES
LEFT TO DIE (Book #1)
LEFT TO RUN (Book #2)
LEFT TO HIDE (Book #3)
LEFT TO KILL (Book #4)
LEFT TO MURDER (Book #5)
LEFT TO ENVY (Book #6)
LEFT TO LAPSE (Book #7)
LEFT TO VANISH (Book #8)
LEFT TO HUNT (Book #9)
LEFT TO FEAR (Book #10)
LEFT TO PREY (Book #11)
LEFT TO LURE (Book #12)
LEFT TO CRAVE (Book #13)
LEFT TO LOATHE (Book #14)
LEFT TO HARM (Book #15)
LEFT TO RUIN (Book #16)

THE AU PAIR SERIES
ALMOST GONE (Book#1)
ALMOST LOST (Book #2)
ALMOST DEAD (Book #3)

ZOE PRIME MYSTERY SERIES
FACE OF DEATH (Book#1)
FACE OF MURDER (Book #2)
FACE OF FEAR (Book #3)

FACE OF MADNESS (Book #4)
FACE OF FURY (Book #5)
FACE OF DARKNESS (Book #6)

A JESSIE HUNT PSYCHOLOGICAL SUSPENSE SERIES
THE PERFECT WIFE (Book #1)
THE PERFECT BLOCK (Book #2)
THE PERFECT HOUSE (Book #3)
THE PERFECT SMILE (Book #4)
THE PERFECT LIE (Book #5)
THE PERFECT LOOK (Book #6)
THE PERFECT AFFAIR (Book #7)
THE PERFECT ALIBI (Book #8)
THE PERFECT NEIGHBOR (Book #9)
THE PERFECT DISGUISE (Book #10)
THE PERFECT SECRET (Book #11)
THE PERFECT FAÇADE (Book #12)
THE PERFECT IMPRESSION (Book #13)
THE PERFECT DECEIT (Book #14)
THE PERFECT MISTRESS (Book #15)
THE PERFECT IMAGE (Book #16)
THE PERFECT VEIL (Book #17)
THE PERFECT INDISCRETION (Book #18)
THE PERFECT RUMOR (Book #19)
THE PERFECT COUPLE (Book #20)
THE PERFECT MURDER (Book #21)
THE PERFECT HUSBAND (Book #22)
THE PERFECT SCANDAL (Book #23)
THE PERFECT MASK (Book #24)

CHLOE FINE PSYCHOLOGICAL SUSPENSE SERIES
NEXT DOOR (Book #1)
A NEIGHBOR'S LIE (Book #2)
CUL DE SAC (Book #3)
SILENT NEIGHBOR (Book #4)
HOMECOMING (Book #5)
TINTED WINDOWS (Book #6)

KATE WISE MYSTERY SERIES

IF SHE KNEW (Book #1)
IF SHE SAW (Book #2)
IF SHE RAN (Book #3)
IF SHE HID (Book #4)
IF SHE FLED (Book #5)
IF SHE FEARED (Book #6)
IF SHE HEARD (Book #7)

THE MAKING OF RILEY PAIGE SERIES
WATCHING (Book #1)
WAITING (Book #2)
LURING (Book #3)
TAKING (Book #4)
STALKING (Book #5)
KILLING (Book #6)

RILEY PAIGE MYSTERY SERIES
ONCE GONE (Book #1)
ONCE TAKEN (Book #2)
ONCE CRAVED (Book #3)
ONCE LURED (Book #4)
ONCE HUNTED (Book #5)
ONCE PINED (Book #6)
ONCE FORSAKEN (Book #7)
ONCE COLD (Book #8)
ONCE STALKED (Book #9)
ONCE LOST (Book #10)
ONCE BURIED (Book #11)
ONCE BOUND (Book #12)
ONCE TRAPPED (Book #13)
ONCE DORMANT (Book #14)
ONCE SHUNNED (Book #15)
ONCE MISSED (Book #16)
ONCE CHOSEN (Book #17)

MACKENZIE WHITE MYSTERY SERIES
BEFORE HE KILLS (Book #1)
BEFORE HE SEES (Book #2)
BEFORE HE COVETS (Book #3)
BEFORE HE TAKES (Book #4)

BEFORE HE NEEDS (Book #5)
BEFORE HE FEELS (Book #6)
BEFORE HE SINS (Book #7)
BEFORE HE HUNTS (Book #8)
BEFORE HE PREYS (Book #9)
BEFORE HE LONGS (Book #10)
BEFORE HE LAPSES (Book #11)
BEFORE HE ENVIES (Book #12)
BEFORE HE STALKS (Book #13)
BEFORE HE HARMS (Book #14)

AVERY BLACK MYSTERY SERIES
CAUSE TO KILL (Book #1)
CAUSE TO RUN (Book #2)
CAUSE TO HIDE (Book #3)
CAUSE TO FEAR (Book #4)
CAUSE TO SAVE (Book #5)
CAUSE TO DREAD (Book #6)

KERI LOCKE MYSTERY SERIES
A TRACE OF DEATH (Book #1)
A TRACE OF MURDER (Book #2)
A TRACE OF VICE (Book #3)
A TRACE OF CRIME (Book #4)
A TRACE OF HOPE (Book #5)